NEVER PLAY
ANOTHER
MAN'S GAME

Also by Mike Knowles

Darwin's Nightmare
Grinder
In Plain Sight

NEVER PLAY ANOTHER MAN'S GAME

MIKE KNOWLES

ECW Press

Published by ECW Press
2120 Queen Street East, Suite 200, Toronto, Ontario, Canada M4E 1E2
416-694-3348 / info@ecwpress.com

Library and Archives Canada Cataloguing in Publication

Knowles, Mike
Never play another man's game / Mike Knowles.

I. Title.

PS8621.N67N48 2012   C813'.6   C2011-906968-7

ISBN: 978-1-77041-097-8
also issued as: 978-1-77090-208-4 (PDF); 978-1-77090-209-1 (ePub)

Cover and Text Design: Tania Craan
Cover Image: © Estefania Abad / Getty Images
Printing: Friesens   5   4   3   2   1

MIX
Paper from
responsible sources
FSC® C016245

The publication of *Never Play Another Man's Game* has been generously supported by the
Canada Council for the Arts which last year invested $20.1 million in writing and publishing
throughout Canada, and by the Ontario Arts Council, an agency of the Government of Ontario. We
also acknowledge the financial support of the Government of Canada through the Canada Book Fund
for our publishing activities, and the contribution of the Government of Ontario through the Ontario
Book Publishing Tax Credit. The marketing of this book was made possible
with the support of the Ontario Media Development Corporation.

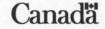
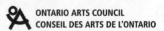

Canada Council   Conseil des Arts
for the Arts   du Canada

Canada

ONTARIO ARTS COUNCIL
CONSEIL DES ARTS DE L'ONTARIO

Printed and bound in Canada

For Andrea.
It could be for no one else.

CHAPTER ONE

The knock came at exactly seven in the morning. I was standing in the kitchen drinking a cup of tea and reading a story in the paper about a kid who had been dragged half a kilometre in a hit and run. The paper had plenty of quotes from the kid's parents, but no answers as to why the fifteen-year-old was out on the street, by himself, at three in the morning. Seven wasn't early for me — I didn't sleep much anymore, but it was too early for someone to be at the door. The knock had a fast beat: three solid knocks in quick succession. After the sounds, a heavy silence settled in like a fog. The quiet was interrupted by the sound of the furnace sputtering to life. The old machinery was struggling to keep up with the November chill.

I put my tea down and walked to the pantry. I had everything from the second shelf on the counter when the second set of knocks on the door sounded. I didn't waste time wondering who was outside — I knew who it was. Not long ago, I killed a cop and a few Russian gangsters. I thought I had gotten out clean, but the knocks said different. It was too early for salesmen, and I had never met one of my neighbours. It had to be the police at the door — Russians don't knock.

I poured three times, not caring about the overflow that soaked the counter. I had just put the metal container down and started corking when a third set of knocks rang out. Something was shouted, but all I picked out was the word "police." The word was distorted from its trip through the door and down the hall, but it was understandable enough.

I had started taping when there was a new sound. The knocking had been replaced with a single sharp noise. Someone thought that they could kick my front door down. I grinned at the image of what had to be going on outside. Someone would be clutching his foot and swearing. The door had about half an inch of an old wooden door glued to the surface of a much more solid metal door. A foot would bounce off the door like bullets off Superman's chest. I had finished taping when something much more substantial hit the door. The sound came a second and then a third time. The third strike was louder than the previous two and I knew the door had started to buckle. I lit the tampon taped to the neck of the one-litre glass bottle and shouldered through the swinging kitchen door when the fourth blow sent the outside door crashing inward. The Molotov was airborne as the first cop stepped inside. The cop only managed to get one foot inside when the corked bottle exploded, sloshing the turpentine inside against the solvent-soaked fiery tampon duct-taped to the neck of the bottle. The patch of wall above the door burst into flames as a spray of liquid fire splashed onto the walls and floor. The police dove for the lawn while I backed into the kitchen.

I had managed to make three Molotov cocktails in under a minute. I kept the bottles, tape, turpentine, lighter, and feminine fuses in the pantry for a special occasion. Most people have food in the kitchen for unexpected company — I kept something for other kinds of visitors. I took the open container of turpentine and pushed the swinging door again. I saw the police on the porch shielding themselves from the flames; they didn't see me toss the can into the hall. The fluid went up in a whoosh as I dashed back the way I came. I lit the second Molotov, threw it against the wall, and the kitchen blossomed into an inferno as I grabbed my coat and slipped into the garage. I got behind the wheel, buckled up, started the engine, and drove straight through the garage door.

The police had parked on the street, not wanting to announce their presence. Their tactical decision gave me enough room to drive across the neighbour's lawn and around the crude roadblock set up in front of the neighbour's house. None of the cops were prepared for a car chase and I saw men running towards cruisers in my rearview as I drove down the street.

The Volvo was a custom job; the exterior was old and worn but the engine under the hood could have almost met drag racing standards. The car was at eighty before I turned the corner and at a hundred by the time I skidded onto the main road. I weaved through the early morning traffic, using the sidewalk as a passing lane, until I saw the first major intersection. I careened around the corner and aimed at the bumper of a Hummer. The black H3 was a scaled-down version of the original design. The new Hummer was for yuppies and assholes, not soldiers. I rear-ended the SUV and felt the seatbelt catch my body as it was thrown forward and then back. I pulled the gun I kept holstered under the seat, lit the last Molotov, and opened the door. The H3 driver was already out of his car with his arms extended in a *what the fuck?* gesture. The

3

anger changed to confusion when he saw me pitch a flaming bottle into my own car. The Volvo was suddenly a fireball and the H3 driver, a fat man in a leather jacket, was backing off. I grabbed him by collar, pressed the gun into his chubby neck right below his Bluetooth ear bud, and forced him back into the SUV. The fat man scrambled over the seat to the passenger side with his hands in the air as I slid into the Hummer. The other motorists and pedestrians were looking back and forth between the Hummer and the flaming Volvo. Some already had cell phones in their hands either to take pictures or to call for help. I put the Hummer in gear and hit the tail end of the green light. I used my elbow to shut up my passenger and then aimed the SUV for the highway.

CHAPTER TWO

ONE WEEK LATER

The Shih Tzu in her arms couldn't have weighed more than two pounds. The pup had matted fur and an underbite. If Ruby Chu liked holding the dog, I couldn't tell. She let the animal lick her hand but pulled away whenever the dog went for her face. The mutt was young, just weeks old, and probably inbred, but it knew the score already. The more affection it showed, the longer it stayed out of the little box it called home. I had picked the pet store in Limeridge Mall for the meet once I had found Ruby. I learned through a friend that she was spreading word, and cash, that she wanted to see me. Ruby and I went way back, but that wasn't why I set up the meet. I didn't owe Ruby Chu a thing; we had lost contact years ago and I was fine with that. I had thought she had been too, but hearing that she was looking for me told me different. I didn't trust her — I had pissed off too many people and pulled too many triggers to think that there was anyone out there who just wanted to catch up. My life was an exercise in invisible minimalism. What remnants of a traceable existence I possessed would be hard to see with a microscope. I could count the people I saw more than once a year on the fingers of my right hand. That made the idea of someone suddenly deciding to look me up hard to accept as coincidence. I set up a meet with Ruby to see who, if anyone, was pulling the strings. Maybe the cops were using her; worse, maybe it was the Russians. I needed to know if someone was hunting me, and to do that I had to do a little hunting myself.

I started by following the whispers. I checked bars and asked about Ruby asking about me. I spread a little money of my own and found out that she was coming around every few days to look for me. The schedule had been steady for over two weeks — too urgent for an old friend looking to catch up. I spent the next two nights watching Sully's Tavern from the mouth of a nearby alley. The spot I chose was home to a Dumpster belonging to an all-day breakfast place. The smell of rotting bits of fried eggs and grease kept people from using the alley as a shortcut or an impromptu place to get high. The garbage even smelled bad enough to keep hungry scavengers away; there were plenty of other places to get a free bite that didn't trigger a gag reflex from ten feet away. The shifts watching the bar door open and close went slow. I spent the first hours of the first shift learning how to relax into the smell. There was no way to avoid it — it was everywhere and any attempt to combat it would just bring attention to me. Instead, I had to accept the smell and let it in. I gradually became able to take deeper and deeper breaths until I was relaxed in the dark and completely invisible.

"It's like that movie with the leather-faced Australian," my uncle had once said.

MIKE KNOWLES

"*Crocodile Dundee*," I said. My uncle never knew the proper names for anything that wasn't directly linked to his wallet or his survival. Over the span of my apprenticeship, I learned to decipher his language of vague clues and basic descriptions.

"Yeah, stupid movie, but there's this one part where the blonde is filling up her canteen at the water's edge."

"I know the part," I said.

"I bet you do, but I ain't talking about her ass, great as it is, I'm talking about the crocodile."

"It attacks her," I said. I had seen the movie dozens of times. I had dropped out of school in favour of becoming a professional thief like my uncle. Instead of learning algebra and biology, I robbed banks and ripped off people who had more money than sense. I had a lot of late nights and *Crocodile Dundee* was a staple of late-night television.

"Yeah, the fucking thing goes for her throat. How's she miss it? It's right there the whole time. Watch the movie, not her ass, and you'll see it. Damn thing is so still, it doesn't matter that it's twelve feet long and a couple hundred pounds. Being still is the same thing as being gone."

It was another lesson I didn't understand right away. I tried to get my head around it, but the stillness he talked about wasn't there. It was the first time in my life that my uncle didn't attempt to beat the rest of the lesson into me. Usually, anything worth teaching had both an oral and a physical component. What was said was reinforced through rigorous repetition and painful examinations. Stillness was a different lesson. The word was whispered again and again while we watched whatever it was we were going to take. Inside a car a block away, my finger would begin to tap on the window and my uncle would whisper one word, "Still." My toe tapping while we opened a bank account in a branch we were about to close for a day would be reprimanded with a quiet, familiar mantra, "Still."

Looking back, I realized that the lesson was something that could never have been beaten into me. Being afraid of a punch, or an elbow, would have never allowed me to be still. I had to learn it on my own. As I remembered each job in my mind, I recalled the subtle changes that took place. Surveillance began in cars blocks away, then moved to watching from across the street. Then the car disappeared and I started watching from crowds. Eventually, I cased jobs alone from distances close enough to hear a whisper. Over time, I had learned to be still.

I waited in the alley, like the crocodile in the movie, for Ruby to stop by the bar for her own drink. When she finally showed up, on the second night, she didn't see me. She checked the alleys and doorways from her side of the street, giving each dark space equal consideration. I watched her look into my hiding space from where she stood and felt no rise in my pulse. I was part of the darkness. Still. Ruby moved on and continued looking around the street. When she was finally happy with what she saw, she walked into Sully's. I stayed where I was and watched the bar. A second later, there was movement in the window and I saw someone looking out at the street. Almost fifteen years since I had seen her and she was still a pro. I watched her check the street again and then I picked up the car I had boosted from the airport parking lot. Forty minutes later, Ruby walked out of the bar; I watched her from under a burnt-out street light. I let the old con woman get around the corner before I started the car and followed.

I was driving a Honda Civic that was way more than five years old. Since losing the Volvo, I had been getting by without a car, but on a job like this wheels were necessary. I had boosted the Civic early that morning; it was a good choice. The grey car was common in the city, fast enough for what I needed, and the thick layer of frost on the windshield meant it had been there at least overnight. I took the car from the airport to the hospital and cruised the underground lot until I found another Civic. I parked nearby, switched plates with the doppelganger, and drove away with a clean vehicle.

I rounded the corner and caught sight of Ruby getting into a red Chevy Malibu. I accelerated and put my high beams on. When I passed Ruby, I watched her look away to avoid the harsh oncoming glare. She wouldn't have been able to identify the make of the car let alone the identity of the driver. I rounded the block and pulled to the curb; a few seconds later, the red Malibu passed by. I rolled away from the curb and fell in behind the Chevy. I followed Ruby to two more bars; she gave each one the same forty minutes that she gave Sully's Tavern. By one a.m., Ruby was on her way out of the downtown core. I followed her off King Street and wound through a few side streets until the Malibu pulled to the curb in front of a small house on Aberdeen. I had already clicked the headlights off when we entered the residential neighbourhood so there weren't any beams of light when I pulled to the curb fifty metres up the street from the Malibu.

Ruby crossed the boulevard and the sidewalk and walked up a short set of stairs leading to a small red brick house. Ruby entered the darkness of the porch and then disappeared into the house. I waited up the street, watching windows light up and go black before the house finally went dark. I pulled away from the curb, gave the car and the house one last look, and then went home.

My eviction the week before had cost me almost every possession I had. All of my tools, clothes, and what money I kept in the house went up in smoke as soon as the flames found the propane tanks I kept upstairs. The papers had done a front-page story on the explosion and the injuries to several police officers, but there wasn't much follow-up. What little the police knew about me atomized when their only lead blew up in their faces. The next day, I had rented a house just outside the core on Queen Street. The landlord, a grumpy painter, rented me the basement and the first floor of his pre-war house for the first two months' overpriced rent up front and in cash. I was fine with paying too much for a little while. The building kept me close to the city and offered both privacy and security — there were two exits to two different streets and a basement door that led to a backyard. I put a new lock on each door to keep the landlord from snooping and made do with the new space. There was nothing to sit on, not even a bed, but the new place would work until I found something more permanent. With the house, I had burned the front I lived behind. It would take some time to build up a new identity to hide under.

I ate, slept, and went back to Ruby's for ten the next night. I took a spot fourteen car-lengths away from the Malibu and watched the house. There were lights on, but I had no way to know if Ruby planned to hit the town again. Ruby had been by two bars after Sully's. I had been by each one after I heard she was looking for me. From what I had heard, she wasn't in every night. That either meant she was checking other places other nights, or that she was working a rotation. I got comfortable in the seat and waited. The November air was frigid and its cold fingers worked their way into the car. I sat in the below-zero silence watching the house. I left the engine off; a car parked on the street with the engine running would attract unwanted attention. I waited until one before I backed out of the space and turned around. I was being extra cautious with Ruby. I didn't want to risk a chance of her seeing my car drive by her house. The sight could easily set off something in her con brain that she would feel as gut instinct. I didn't want to give her any warning. I wanted her thinking she was the one doing the looking so that she would never see me coming.

I was back the next night just in time to see Ruby leave. The Malibu pulled away from the curb with a screech of tires and tore down the street. I didn't follow the car; instead, I stayed where I was and watched the house. For twenty minutes, I watched the windows. All of the lights were off and no one opened the curtains to look at the street. At ten thirty, I got out of the car and walked towards the house on the opposite sidewalk. I passed Ruby's place and crossed the street when I reached the park a half a kilometre up the road. I walked down the other side of the street watching for any nosey homeowners who might be peering into the street from their living rooms. When I was sure that I was not being watched, I turned off the sidewalk and walked over the lawn to the side of Ruby's house. The space between the house and the neighbours was separated by a six-foot-tall wooden fence. The solid fence, and the lack of a light on the side of the house, made picking the lock easy. No one noticed me crouching beside the reinforced metal door. The lock took thirty seconds to turn.

I opened the door and stepped inside unafraid of tripping an alarm system. Ruby was a grifter — she ran cons, picked pockets, and committed every type of fraud imaginable — so she would never want the law in her house even if she were the victim of a crime. I checked for an alarm just in case, but I was right. I then checked if anyone else was home. All of the lights in the house were off, but that didn't mean the house was clear — someone could have been sleeping. I checked each room and found no one catching zzzs. The house was empty and there were only size-four clothes in the closets. Ruby lived alone. Throughout the house was picture after picture of Ruby with a young boy. In each picture, the boy got bigger and older until the boy maxed out and no longer grew. I'd never known that Ruby had a kid.

I walked away from the frames and began a deeper search of the house. I found money stashed in a coffee can in the freezer, a gun under the mattress, and several fake pieces of ID with the same woman's face on them. I also found three wigs in the bathroom. All three were the same colour and the same length — each just in a slightly different style. Inside the medicine cabinet, I found more pill bottles than any person should have. I also found a daily pill dispenser. I popped open the pill slot for the next day and saw that Ruby would be taking twelve pills on Tuesday. I didn't recognize any of the names etched on the pills, but the cancer pamphlets on the night table filled me in.

Ruby had lung cancer. To fight the disease, she had been going through radiation and chemo. The pamphlets listed hair loss as a possible side effect; the wigs confirmed it as a definite. I went back into the bathroom and looked at the wigs. Beside the three, there was a fourth Styrofoam head that was bald. This was the style that Ruby had chosen for the night. I pulled the folded piece of paper from my pocket, placed it in front of the head under a prepaid cell that I had bought the day before, and then I walked out the door.

The next day, I tailed Ruby to Limeridge Mall. She drove a lot more carefully and checked behind her a lot more often after she had found my note, but it didn't matter — I was able to stay far behind her because I had the advantage of knowing exactly where she was going. Ruby parked where I had told her to and went into the mall.

MIKE KNOWLES

I followed her inside and waited for her to sit down in the food court. From the second floor, I could see down into the dining area. Ruby sat alone for five minutes; she did nothing to signal anyone. She looked a lot like I remembered. But now, she looked more like the older sister of the petite Asian woman of my memories. She wore jeans and a hooded sweatshirt. On her shoulder, she carried a large leather purse. The jet-black wig she wore had been on the second Styrofoam head the night before. It must have been an expensive wig because I would have never noticed it was faux hair had I not been inside her house.

I opened the matching disposable prepaid cell phone I had bought and dialled Ruby. I watched her react to the ring tone I set and then I watched her fish around in her purse for the phone.

"Hello?"

"Meet me in the pet store on the second floor. Ask to hold the Shih Tzu."

"Wilson?" Out of her mouth, my name still carried the slight trace of the accent she could never seem to shake.

I hung up and watched her realize that she was no longer speaking to me. She looked angrily at the phone and then put it away in the big bag. A few seconds later, Ruby was on her feet and on her way to the escalator. The second floor of the mall had stores on opposite sides with railings overlooking the floor below between them. I watched Ruby from the other side of the mall as she walked. She kept checking her blind spots, but I was never in them — I was walking in front of her the whole time on the opposite side. I watched through gaps in the crowd as her pace slowed. Ruby pulled out another cell phone, this one from a pocket, and began texting with one hand. Whatever the message was, it was brief. Ruby slid the phone back in her pocket and picked up the pace again. When she went into

Petropolis, I went into a health food store on the other side of the mall. Through the glass, I watched her talk to the sales associate. The young girl walked away from her and Ruby looked around the store aimlessly until the dog appeared. Ruby was led to a bench next to a door leading to the back room of the pet store. Ruby held the dog for five minutes. I used the time to watch the store. I didn't see anyone else giving the pet store any attention. Five minutes is a long time — if Ruby had a tail they would have at least done a few walk-bys. The old woman gave up on the dog and the meet when the puppy peed on her. I watched her hand the Shih Tzu back to the sales associate and stand up, obviously frustrated. The young saleswoman opened the door to the back room and took the puppy back to its cell. Ruby was still looking at the stain on her shirt when I took her by the arm and led her into the back room after the dog.

14

CHAPTER THREE

The sales associate came back around the corner — this time without a dog in her hands. I kept my hand on Ruby's bicep and my eyes on the rest of her. My left hand produced a fifty, and the clerk took it without stopping.

"Thanks, Becky," I said.

"Anytime."

The girl walked out to the sales floor leaving Ruby and me alone.

"You can let go of me now," Ruby said. Her voice set off the dogs in the cages around us. There were high-pitched barks and pathetic yelps everywhere.

I pulled Ruby to another door. The back door of the store had a warning sign taped to it. Without a key, opening the door would set off an alarm and attract mall security. Becky had left the key in the lock — the reason why I had to pay fifty instead of twenty. We went through the door and ended up in a hallway. The hall ran behind every store in the second floor of the mall, and the businesses used it for taking garbage out. I pulled Ruby to the freight elevator and touched the down button. The door opened immediately and I shoved the old grifter inside. Her purse stayed with me in the hallway. I put the bag on the concrete floor and stepped into the elevator car with Ruby.

"What the hell? Give me my purse, Wilson."

I shook my head and kept my body between her and the door. Most women keep their wallet in their purse, along with their keys and a little makeup. Ruby wasn't most women; she was dangerous when I met her and I doubted she'd got soft in her old age. The bag stayed on the ground. Ruby's little fists balled in frustration, but she stayed where she was. I hit the button with a faded number one in the centre and heard the doors close. When the elevator started moving to the first floor, I said, "How have you been, Ruby?"

"You know how I've been. You broke into my house."

"I'm sorry about the cancer," I said. I had no feelings about it, but it seemed like the thing to say.

"Too many years sitting in that damn bingo hall."

I nodded. I remembered Ruby as an addict. Her disease was worse than being hooked on pills or the bottle. At least with substance abuse you get drunk or high and you get a break from the gnawing inside. With gambling there was no relief. Ruby gambled more when she was winning because she had to take advantage of the hot streak, and she kept on gambling when she was losing because she always thought she could make the money back. She'd play any game of chance that gave her the opportunity to win. I remembered going with my uncle to find her for a job. He drove us to a bingo hall, Ruby's drug of choice. If I closed my eyes, I could still see the blue smoke hanging from the ceiling. If those conditions existed on a job site, Ruby would have had grounds for a lawsuit, but they didn't happen on the job — they happened in a place Ruby chose to visit every night of the week. She sat there for hours with more cards than anyone should have been able to keep track of until the poison around the ceiling found a way into her cells.

"You turned out just like him, you know."

"Who?" I said.

"Your uncle. He would have searched the house too, but he wouldn't have pulled a stunt like this. He knew who his friends were."

"And look where that got him," I said.

"I did what you told me. I met you at the mall, then at the pet store. I don't deserve to be dragged around like this."

"Who'd you text, Ruby?"

"What?"

I pointed at her pocket. "When you were walking through the mall. On the phone in your pocket. Who did you text?"

Ruby Chu laughed at me. It wasn't the laugh of an enemy; it was a genuine sound. "My God, you are just like him. I texted my son, all right? That's who I texted."

"I saw his picture. Seems a bit old to still be needing calls from his mommy."

The elevator door opened and Ruby reached around me and pressed the button for the second floor. I took a step back and stood in between the doors. I felt them touch me and then retract into their housing.

"First of all," Ruby said, "you're never too old to get a call from your mother. And second, I had to let him know we were meeting."

"Why?"

"I wanted him to know that everything is going to be alright."

The doors tried to close again and for the second time, they bounced off my shoulders.

"You have thirty seconds to get my attention. If you don't, I'm gone and we never see each other again."

"I need a man for a job."

"Put an ad in the paper."

"I need a planner to set it up and oversee it. What your uncle used to do."

"He's dead," I said.

"I know."

"So he doesn't do that anymore."

"You're just like him. You could do it."

"I haven't done that kind of work in a while."

Ruby nodded and crossed her arms. "I heard you went to work for the mob."

"It's not that simple," I said.

"It never is, but I hear you don't work for them any-more. Is that simple enough?"

I nodded.

"So you need a job."

"I'm not broke," I said. It was the truth. I lost some money with the house, but I still had reserves stashed all over the city. Not enough to live on, but enough to coast for a while.

"I don't mean it that way. You need a job. What are you going to do? Retire? Get a real job? Settle down? We both know that isn't going to happen. I've lived this life long enough to know that if you aren't working a job, you're looking for one. What else is there for people like us?"

Thirty seconds had passed and I hadn't moved. The door hit me a third time; a sensor must have been triggered because there was suddenly an annoying buzzer coming from the elevator. I stepped inside and the doors had luck on the fourth try.

"You don't know me, Ruby."

"No? I knew your uncle, and I see him in you. He couldn't stop either."

"And it got him dead."

"So what was the alternative? You know what happens to the animals at Sea World when they get taken out of the ocean and put in those big tanks?"

"They get a steady diet of fish and no one ever gets caught in a net again."

Ruby shook her head. "They get ulcers. Some of them have to go on a steady diet of antacids. Others start hurting themselves, or picking fights with a fish that will do it for them."

"But they stay alive."

"They're not alive, they're just waiting to die. Some just figure out how to make it happen faster than others. Working is dangerous, sure, but it's our life. People like us were never meant to dance for sardines three times a day for a little safety. The sooner you come to terms with that, the better."

The doors opened on the second floor and Ruby's purse was still there. I picked it up and pushed the button for the first floor. "We get a cup of coffee and talk the job over. If I think the job has legs, I'll stick around. If the job is bullshit, no story about Flipper will make me stay. I'd rather jump for sardines than share a cell in the Kingston Pen."

Ruby reached into her pocket. I took the cell out of her hand the second she had it out.

"I just want to tell my son what's going on. He'll worry."

"Concentrate on talking to me," I said.

CHAPTER FOUR

We sat in a small coffee house just down the street from a hospital near the mall. There were only four tables and a couch for the patrons. I drank black tea with milk while Ruby nursed a cup of green tea.

"My son came to me with the job. A friend of his does maintenance for an armoured car company and my son found out that the trucks are going in one by one because of some repairs they need."

Ruby paused as though she were offering me a chance to ask a question. I said nothing and kept my face blank. I wanted Ruby to tell the story, the whole story, her way. She hadn't started the way most people did. Most people start a job proposal with money. They tell you how much you'll make right off the bat, so that you're already spending it in your head while you hear the rest of the story. Greed makes people go against their better judgement; it makes people sign on to jobs they should have run from. Telling me about an inside man was a bad way to start. It showed that Ruby had no idea how much money was to be made. Worse, it was an immediate red flag. Inside knowledge meant there was already a civilian involved. Civilians are never part of a good job. Involving them increases the chances of failure exponentially and they are the first to squeal when the police sweat them at the station. Civilians have more to lose than professionals, so they'll take whatever deal is on the table and feel no shame in it.

"The company this guy works for," Ruby went on, "they do some bank work, but they mostly do a lot of replenishing ATMs. Because one of the trucks is down each week for maintenance, they have been doubling up routes every Friday. One truck does its normal route, and then it's supposed to drive back to the warehouse to load up for the second route. It's a long double shift. Good money. The drivers doing the work decided that cutting out lunch and stuffing the truck with cash for both routes is worth the hassle. They rush the job so they can make it back to the warehouse for a Friday night poker game. They put in a few hours playing cards while they make time and a half and then punch out and go home."

She paused again. I said nothing.

"So that's it. We got a full truck rolling around ripe for the picking."

Ruby leaned back in her chair and took a sip of tea. She looked pleased with herself. Her smile slowly vanished when she saw that I didn't share her enthusiasm.

"C'mon, Wilson. It's an armoured car filled to the brim. This should be right up your alley."

"You think this is right up my alley?"

"It's not? I remember hearing about a few armoured cars that ended up empty because of you and your —"

I raised a finger. "First off, you got a tip on the maintenance schedule. How did you come by the information?"

"I told you, my son knows a guy."

"How well does he know him? Better yet, how well does this guy know your kid?"

Ruby didn't say anything.

"So, we're going on second-hand information. What happens when the truck gets knocked over and the police turn up? And they will turn up. The cops will be looking hard at the employees, because the robbery is going to stink like an inside job. How else would someone know the exact right day and car to rob? They'll have questions for everyone, especially the mechanic. Is this source cut into the deal? Does he have a reason to keep his mouth shut? More importantly, is he the kind of guy who can handle an interview with a cop without giving everything up?"

Ruby didn't say anything. She was quiet because she didn't know the answers.

"Second," I said as I ticked off another finger. "Repairs to armoured trucks can't last forever. Your boy found out presumably after the repairs had already started and it took you some time to find me. That leaves us with little time to plan and even less to get what we would need to do the job. Armoured car isn't just a clever name, Ruby. They don't break open easy and getting the necessary tools to bust the piggy bank is a hell of a lot tougher since 9/11. You start buying explosives through the wrong channels and you'll be waving at the cops while the Mounties take you away."

I drank some of my tea, which was not as hot as I liked, and then raised a third finger. "Lastly, I didn't hear a figure come out of your mouth. You just know that the truck has more money inside than usual. What's usual? Will double cover the expenses and still make it worthwhile when we split up the take?"

Ruby had stopped looking so pleased with herself. "You won't do it, then?"

"Jesus, Ruby, this isn't like agreeing to help someone move. This has got bad idea written all over it. You don't see that?"

Ruby picked up her tea and then put it down without drinking any. She avoided making eye contact and tried to nonchalantly rub at her eyes.

I drained the last of my lukewarm tea and put the cup down. "Ruby, you're a grifter. You run cons and scams. What the hell are you doing going after an armoured car?"

She stopped fidgeting and looked at me; her eyes were filled with tears just waiting to jump.

"It's my son. He needs the money."

"Tell me everything," I said.

"He's into some people for a lot of money."

"Gambling?" I asked.

Ruby looked at the floor and nodded. "Poker." She was ashamed that her son had inherited her vice.

"How much?"

Ruby shook her head. "Just under a hundred. He doesn't have the money and neither do I. I already paid his debts once. The cancer took care of what I had left. I don't have a drug plan and the medicine that makes me look so goddamn ravishing isn't free. I'm pretty much down to the house and a few wigs."

Her kid being in debt made the whole deal even worse. People who owe big to bad people do stupid, unpredictable shit. Worse, you already know they're a liability because smart people don't get in over their heads with loan sharks.

"So, he's in deep and you're cleaned out. His solution is to knock over an armoured car."

Ruby nodded. "I know it seems like a bad idea, but he's desperate. The money is there and he's going to do the job no matter what. I can't stop my son; I lost control of him years ago. That's why I gave him money the first

24

MIKE KNOWLES

time. I didn't want him to get into more trouble, and I felt responsible. It was my fault he started gambling in the first place. I tried to talk him out of robbing the armoured car, but he won't listen. I thought if I could get someone involved, someone like you, who knows what he's doing, then maybe you could make it work. Make it so my son doesn't go to jail, or worse."

"It's got bad written all over it, Ruby. You've got a stake in it, but me — I'm not signing on for your kid."

"I can pay you to help plan the job. Like a consultant."

"Pay me how, Ruby? You said yourself that you don't have any money, and I don't have any faith in your boy being able to pay me after he does the job. Just let it go. Forget about me and start putting all your energy into talking your boy out of doing this job."

I got up and threw a five-dollar tip down on the table. If Ruby was as hard up as she said, she could steal it before she left.

"Bye, Ruby."

I got to the door when I felt a hand on my arm. Ruby had a hell of a grip for a woman sick with cancer.

"I can give you the house."

"What?"

"I read the paper. I remember that house, Wilson. I know what happened. I can replace what you lost. I can give you my house when I die. If you plan the job, you can have it. He gets the money, maybe, but you for sure get the house."

"Why not sell it and give the money to your son?"

"He doesn't have time to wait for the house to sell. In this market, in that location, a sale would take months. He needs the money now."

I thought about the house. I didn't know much about real estate, but I knew the house was worth well over a hundred grand — a hell of a payday for a consultant. That was if I sold it; the house was worth more to me as a place to live. A place, if I did the right paperwork, that would never have my real name attached to it.

"Tell your son I want to follow the truck around on its delivery route. He needs to be along for the ride. Have him get a hold of me tonight on the cell I gave you."

Ruby brightened. "Thank you, Wilson. Thank you."

She hugged me tight and I felt how frail she was under her clothes.

"What's his name?" I said as I backed out of the hug.

"Rick. I named him Rick."

She looked at me funny when she said it, like we were sharing an inside joke.

"After my uncle?" I asked.

"After his father," she said.

MIKE KNOWLES

The phone rang at nine thirty. I was sitting in a folding chair in my apartment watching an all-news channel while I cleaned my Glock, both chair and TV were recent acquisitions from a downtown pawn shop. I looked at the cell and heard it chime a second time. My hand extended halfway to the phone and hung there. If Ruby had been speaking the truth, the only living relative I had was on the other end of the phone.

I had spent the day thinking about what she had said. She named the kid after his father. It was possible my uncle could have been the father of Ruby's child. Ruby was around often enough when I was younger. She ran with the same crowds and she kept the same hours. If my uncle was going to knock anyone up, it would have been someone like Ruby. I hadn't given her a reaction. Ruby was a world-class con and being around her put me on guard. I wasn't going to give her an inch and I suspected everything she said. She had held her best card close to the vest until the last second, and then she dropped it when she thought it would make the biggest impact. I wasn't dumb enough to think it was just happenstance. With someone like Ruby, there was only cold calculation at work. I went over our conversation again and again, picking at each word she used. She had dropped her bomb after I had agreed to plan the job for her kid. There had to be a benefit to telling me then. If she had told me right away, I would have discounted her revelation as manipulative bullshit. Thinking she was just trying to lure me into the job by appealing to my sense of family would have tainted the job. I would have walked away without looking back.

You're just like him. She had said that more than once. Planting the seeds. Bringing him up, knowing that I would counter with the fact that my uncle was dead. She knew I had no one left and she wanted that fact to be fresh in my mind. She let the idea fester while she tried to convince me into taking the job. Had she been working me the whole time? Were the vague details and shitty plan just a feint before the real punch? Was there some con hiding just below the surface? I fucking hated grifters. Nothing was as it seemed, especially the price you would pay when someone came collecting.

I thought about disappearing, taking off and leaving Ruby to find some other pawn, but Ruby was right about one thing. Like all good con artists, Ruby put a sliver of truth in her pitch, and that stuck in my brain like a splinter. I had tried once to get away, to leave behind the life I grew up in. But the life found me and dragged me home. I had done too much wrong to too many of the wrong kind of people to ever get away clean. What I knew, what Ruby seemed to know too, was that being a regular person would never be for me. It felt like wearing a Halloween mask for too long. I began to itch under the fake skin. The itch kept spreading until it was all I could feel.

I was close to pulling the mask off myself before my old boss showed up and did it for me. Paolo Donati had used me as a fixer for years. He gave me a problem he had and I grinded it out, no questions asked. When his nephews vanished, and he thought his own people were the ones saying abracadabra, I was the only avenue he had left. The avenue turned out to be a dead end. I did the job I was forced to do, but I didn't go back to my old boss. I hated being regular, but I hated being blackmailed more. I did the job and then I settled things with my old boss.

I was done being on a leash — no more mobs, no more crooked cops putting me on a hook. The only problem was money. It wasn't just the house that went up in the fire — it was a life. It would take time and a lot of money to build up another cover as solid as the one I lost when the cops kicked down my door. I had reserves, but nowhere near the amount I needed. If I wanted to stay off someone else's payroll, I had to start earning on my own. I hated the fact that I needed the money. I had seen too many people go down because they were too desperate to say no to a job that had bad written all over it in permanent marker. I wanted to think I was better than those men, but was I compromised? Was my judgement so far off the mark that I wouldn't see the noose coming over my head? I shook my head — those kind of questions were for men with fat wallets and for stupid invincible kids who knew everything. I didn't have the luxury to turn down work — I needed the job. With the house Ruby put up, I could start turning back the clock and become what I was before the mob, before my uncle died — an independent operator. I smiled at the prospect of owing no one and depending on nothing but myself; it seemed natural. It seemed right. Ruby spoke the truth in the coffee shop: I was just like my uncle.

The phone rang a third time. My hand escaped whatever

paralysis held it in limbo and swiped the phone off the milk crate I was using as a coffee table. I pressed talk and put the phone to my ear. There was a bit of distortion, but the loud music on the other end still managed to rush out of the speaker.

"Hello?" a voice said over the music.

"Who gave you this number?" I said.

"Is this . . ."

"No names," I said. "Answer the question without using a name. Who gave you this number?"

"My mother. She said you were on board for this job."

I let the words "on board" go. I wasn't on board with anything. My role was all theoretical. I would put my two cents in and the kid could take it or leave it.

"We on?"

"Sure, the truck leaves from —"

"Easy, Tiger, it was a yes or no question."

"Man, are you paranoid. Do you have a tinfoil helmet on because you worry about the government stealing your thoughts?"

"No worries, just a habit of wanting to stay out of a cell and the ability to handle my affairs without the help of my mommy."

"Hey, fuck you! You don't want in on my job, then get lost."

"Sounds like mommy didn't update you on how things are going to work."

"Stop calling her my mommy. She told me about you. Told me you were a pro, but let's get one thing straight. This is my job, asshole, and if you don't like it you can fuck off."

I grinned and hung up the phone. The kid was worse than I thought he would be. I had hoped, being the kid of a pro like Ruby, he would have inherited a bit more savvy.

Instead, he sounded as green as a kid on the way to his first stay in juvie.

Rick's mom had worked me. She wanted me on the job and she got what she was after. It didn't matter that taking the job felt like it was my own decision; I knew enough to realize that Ruby had pulled me into something with subtle manipulation and expert mind games even if I couldn't see all the strings at work. Getting the kid to call me was my way of pushing the game in a different direction. Ruby was playing doubles now and she was teamed with a shitty partner. I wanted to see how she would handle the rebound. I turned the news back up and got back to cleaning the gun. I had finished with the gun and was dozing in my chair when the phone rang again. I answered on the second ring and heard Ruby's voice.

"I'm sorry," she said.

"Don't be. The kid laid everything out for me. He told me if I wasn't on board, I could fuck off, so I fucked."

"He's young and impetuous."

"He's a fucking amateur who doesn't know enough to not use names over the phone. He's going to get himself arrested or dead."

"That's why we need you. We have no one to help us. You're all we have."

The obvious implication was that they were all I had, too. Ruby's manipulations were getting easier to spot. I didn't want a family business — I had that once and it didn't last, but I did want the house. If I was going to get the property, I had to do my part, and to do that I would also need a little help from Rick.

"You want my help, then explain the deal to your boy. If he goes for it, meet me in the parking lot outside where we met this morning. You drive so I'll know you weren't followed."

"I can't come tomorrow. I have an appointment with my . . . hairdresser."

Bald women don't get their hair done — Ruby meant her oncologist.

"Reschedule it. I want you there."

"I can't."

"Six a.m.," I said and hung up the phone.

was in the mall parking lot at four thirty in the morning. The car I was sitting in was another "rental" from the airport. The black Volkswagen Passat was just old enough, and expensive enough, to go unnoticed in plain sight. Someone looking at the car would figure it belonged where it was because what crook would drive a nice safe sedan like that. I parked in the far corner of the lot near several other cars. The mall parking lot was a hub for carpooling, making it easy to blend in.

I sat low in the seat and watched the lot. Other carpoolers showed up and left, mall cleaning staff rolled in, and at six, a red Malibu entered the lot. The car drove towards the entrance to the food court and did a wide circle around the lot. The Malibu passed the small pack of cars I was parked in, but it didn't stop. When I lifted my head above the dash, I saw that the Malibu had Ruby behind the wheel and a much taller man riding shotgun. Both were moving their heads left and right looking for my car. The Malibu did a second lap before choosing a space in the middle of the lot.

Thirty seconds passed and then my cell phone rang. I let it go and watched the lot. For fifteen minutes, I let the Malibu sit there. The cell phone kept ringing and I kept waiting. No other cars came into the lot and no one walked or jogged by. Satisfied Ruby and Rick came alone, I started the Volkswagen and drove to the space next to the Malibu. Ruby looked thin and tired. Instead of a wig, she wore a kerchief tied around her head. The man beside her leaned forward so that he could see me and I saw that he didn't look tired — he looked pissed.

Rick looked to be in his mid-twenties. He had thick black hair that he combed high on his head and a faint bit of stubble under his nose and on his chin. He got out of the car fast and circled around the VW's hood. He was a big man, easily six feet, and he looked like he had some size under his hooded jacket. He slammed his palm down on the hood of the car and yelled, "Get out, motherfucker!"

Ruby opened her door and got out of the car. She spoke quietly and I couldn't make out what she said. Rick swatted at the air like there was a bee near his face and shouted, "Get back in the car, Mom!"

Ruby said something else, this time louder; I caught a few of the words. Rick turned his head and started to say something back when my foot moved off the brake and mashed the accelerator. The Volkswagen covered the three feet of asphalt between Rick and the hood in a second and hit him just above the knees. Rick's body was bent at the waist and his chest collided with the hood of the car. This time I heard Ruby loud and clear when she screamed her son's name.

I yanked the emergency brake back and got out of the car just in time to see Rick slide off the hood. The impact was enough to bruise and scare — I doubted that I broke anything.

"My fuckin' leg."

The early morning November air felt good on my face. The black watch cap I wore and the turned-up collar on my peacoat kept the cold from getting in anywhere else.

Ruby knelt beside her son. She was feeling his legs and asking him if he was alright.

"No, I'm not alright. This psycho hit me with his goddamn car."

"Can you get up?"

"I think so, Ma, but it hurts real bad."

"Then get in the car," she said.

I said nothing while Rick got off the ground using the Passat's hood for support. He called me an asshole and then limped towards the Malibu.

"The other car," Ruby said.

"What?"

"Get in his car. I'll sit in the back so you can stretch your legs."

"Are you fucking serious? I'm really hurt."

Ruby nodded and opened the passenger door. Rick limped back to the VW; this time, each step was followed by a sharp intake of breath just in case we didn't realize he was hurt. Rick got in without looking at me. When the door closed, Ruby said, "Was that really necessary?"

"You kept telling me how much I'm like my uncle. How would he have dealt with that?"

Ruby looked at the hood and then at the pavement. There was no blood or missing teeth anywhere.

"Maybe you're not so much like him."

"Get in the car," I said.

I opened the door and got behind the wheel. Ruby got in behind her kid and then slid over so that she was behind my seat because Rick had moved his seat as far back as it would go. He had pulled his pant legs up so he could inspect his knees. He did a lot of prodding and wincing.

"Comfortable?"

"Fuck you."

"That's the spirit," I said as I exited the parking lot. "Tell me where I'm going."

"The truck starts on the Stoney Creek Mountain and does its regular route filling grocery store ATMs. The guys skip their lunch and then go to Walmarts all over the city to set up their bank machines for the weekend."

"They do this every day?"

"They do stuff for banks and other businesses too, but Monday and Friday is always ATMs."

"And Friday is the best day?"

"There's no guarantee on what they're carrying other days. The Friday route is for sure double the usual. My leg really hurts. I think I cracked something. Ma, do you have any Tylenol?"

Ruby said, "Let me check, baby."

"Who's feeding you this?"

"None of your business, that's who." Rick took some pills from his mom and said, "What no water?"

"Sorry."

"You know I hate dry swallowing pills. They get stuck in my throat every time."

"Sorry, honey."

Out of the corner of my eye, I watched Rick cock his head back to propel the pills down his throat. A second later, he said, "See? Great! The goddamn things are stuck. I told you this would happen, Ma. I told you."

"Rick, how do you know about the trucks?"

"What did I say?"

"It's a friend he went to high school with. He does the mechanical work on all of the trucks."

"Ma!"

"This guy know what Rick plans to do with the information he gave him?"

"Don't talk about me like I'm not here. My buddy was out for drinks with his co-workers in Hess Village. He bumped into me and some people I was partying with and we hung out for a while. He got super shitfaced and started talking business in the john. I heard him when I was in the stall taking a shit."

I looked at Ruby in the rear-view mirror. "It just keeps getting better and better," I said.

"What the fuck does that mean?"

"It means I should have killed you with the car and put you out of your misery."

"Ma-aa!" The word came out whiny like he was complaining I wouldn't share.

"I've seen the route, Wilson. It's better than it sounds."

"Uh hunh."

"It is, asshole," Rick said. "You'll see."

Rick guided me to the parking lot of a huge grocery store. The Market was part of a chain that had sprouted locations across southern Ontario over the last few years. I pulled into a spot that gave us a clear view of the main entrance. I cracked the windows and killed the engine.

"What the hell, man? It's freezing. Roll them up."

I checked the lot and ignored the complaint.

"You hear me? Roll the windows up. Ma, tell him."

"It keeps the glass from fogging up," Ruby said.

Rick crossed his arms over his chest. "I'm just saying. It's cold. There's no need to freeze to death."

"Maybe you should do less saying and more listening," I said.

"Maybe you should remember who scored you this job."

I turned my head so I could look at Rick. He was

rubbing his knee and it took him a second to realize that I was staring at him.

"Right now your job is nothing more than a bit of drunken bathroom gossip. That little bit of knowledge is all you brought to the table. You can't call that a job. If it was a job, your mother wouldn't have found me. This thing will only become a job when I say it does, so sit there and shut up or I'll have your mother wash your mouth out."

Rick started to muster a protest, but Ruby's hand touched his shoulder. "Don't, baby. We need his help."

I chuckled to myself. The kid couldn't have been more of a pussy if he tried.

We had been in the parking lot almost an hour when The Market finally opened its doors for business. Rick did nothing but fidget and bitch the whole time. He whined about being cold, about being sore, and finally about having to pee. I made him use the bathroom in the Wendy's five hundred metres away from the grocery store. He put up a fight and I let his mother explain that going into the place you were casing was a bad idea. When he finally understood, he got out of the car with a lot of complaining. He limped towards the restaurant and I watched him go. The limp slowly dissolved as Rick got farther away from the car. By the time he got to the Wendy's, he was walking fine. When I turned my head towards Ruby, she said, "You don't have to say it."

"But I'm going to."

She sat back in the seat. "Fine."

"Ruby, you know he can't do this job. He's not made for it. I could map the thing out from start to finish and he'd still fuck it up. He's probably already started. I'm betting he's already been hanging around the grocery store attracting all kinds of attention."

"It's all my fault," she said. "He never had a father growing up and I spoiled him."

"You mean you ignored him while you gambled," I said.

I saw her face in the rear-view and the reflection sneered back at me for the briefest of seconds. I had touched a nerve. Ruby's gambling had always been a problem. I could remember my uncle always knowing where to find her. She'd be playing cards in some back room or sitting in some bingo hall every time he needed her. She was always pissed when we showed up, because we were cooling her hot streak or we were bothering her when she was just about to turn things around.

"The kid's got your disease, but he's got a worse strain than you. He plays bigger stakes and he doesn't have your skills. He can rack up debt like a pro, but he can't earn enough to pay his debts. You could always cover your losses well enough, but you can't do double duty, especially when part of that is Rick's debt."

"So what are you saying?"

"I'm saying the ship is sinking and it's time to get in a lifeboat."

"I can't do that. He's my flesh and blood. I can't give up on him. You know what would happen?"

"Who's he owe?"

"Big River." Ruby said the words quietly as though they were heavy on her tongue.

I whistled a low note. Rick liked to lose his money in Toronto poker games instead of bingo halls. The Big River triad planted their flag in Chinatown over a decade ago and wasted no time in assimilating the different local tongs that held on to small pockets of turf around the city. In a few years, Big River had organized a network that ran across the entire province. The triad started small, focussing on

NEVER PLAY ANOTHER MAN'S GAME

gambling and illegal imports, but as their influence grew so did their greed. The triad figured out sneaking in drugs and guns was about as easy as getting knockoff Prada bags past customs. And when they perfected their smuggling routes, people were the last innovation. Why bring in a purse you can sell once at a discount price, when you can bring in a person who will spend years working at sweatshop wages to pay for their freedom at a hugely inflated price? Better still, that same person would then pay the same thing over and over again to bring their relatives to Canada. The fine hand-stitching on a faux purse had nothing on the tight weave of a heartstring stretched across the ocean.

The triad had diversified, but they never gave up on what brought them to the dance. They took their gambling seriously and they took debts with even less humour. If Rick was in deep to Big River, the triad would hurt him, not enough to cripple, but bad enough for him to know they meant business. When he still didn't come up with the money, they'd make an example of him. It would be splashy and it would probably last a weekend.

"You might be better off skipping town."

"I'm dying. I get treatments a couple times a week. I can't just pack up and go. If I did, I wouldn't have to pack much. Where would that leave Rick? He can't survive without me."

"So your only option is to pull a job that will settle the bill."

"You got it."

"You know he won't learn his lesson. He'll just rack up another debt thinking he's badass enough to pay the tab with some more weekend gunplay."

"You're not a parent, so you wouldn't understand. When you're a mom, you'll do anything for your kids. You'll pay any price to keep them safe. It doesn't matter if they'll do the same wrongs again, you'll always be there."

I said nothing.

"I told you, you wouldn't understand," she said.

I kept my mouth shut and pointed. The truck had just pulled into the lot.

CHAPTER SEVEN

One guard got out of the passenger side and walked around to the back of the truck. He knocked on the door and another guard opened it up from the inside. The guard stepped out from the rear, holding a blue duffel bag. The two men did a quick scan of the lot that was more habit than on-the-job vigilance, and then went inside. The duffel had shrink-wrapped bricks of cash inside. The guards would open the ATM and pull out the depleted cassette. One man would stand guard while the other refilled the cassette with the cash from the bag. The stopwatch in my hand said the door was open for twenty-five seconds. The two men entered the store, leaving the driver out front in the truck. The driver waited patiently in the cab and kept busy by checking his mirrors every few seconds.

Two and a half minutes in, Rick got back in the car. He was jazzed up seeing the truck and he gave me a playful punch on the shoulder.

"See, man? Everything I said was on the money. You

doubted me, but you gotta give it to me. I came through, right?"

I didn't take my eyes off the truck. The driver was giving each mirror equal attention. He was alert and professional at his first stop; odds were he would get more and more lax as the day went on. Problem was, the cash would diminish along with the driver's attentiveness. If the truck was going to get hit, it was best to do it early.

At the seven-minute mark, the two guards were back. The back door was opened with keys and the empty duffel bag went in along with one of the guards. The other guard let himself into the passenger seat and the driver started the engine. The driver checked his mirrors and the truck moved away from the curb. I stayed behind the truck, keeping the Volkswagen ten car-lengths away.

The next stop, a Walmart, went much like the first. The two men went in while the driver stayed in the truck checking his mirrors. Two more stops came and went with nothing changing but locations. It was on the fifth stop that something different happened. It was a small difference, but it was something. Stop five, an ATM at a Best Buy, happened without any compulsive mirror checking. The driver instead answered a phone call and stayed on the phone until the other guard let himself back into the cab. From my spot across the lot, it looked like the driver was embarrassed at being caught on the phone. The driver did a quick mirror check, too fast to really notice anything, and got back on the road again with us in tow.

Because the truck was doing a double shift, there was a brief stop for lunch at a Subway restaurant. The guard riding shotgun and the guy in back got out and went in to buy lunch. When they got back, the driver went in, used the washroom, and got a sandwich. The truck was stopped for less than ten minutes and then it was on its way down the Escarpment. The truck did the second half of its run, which included a number of Walmarts and several more supermarkets. Ruby and I took turns getting out of the car and watching the action inside. We had seen everything we were going to see with the driver; we still needed to check the guards for holes in their game. By seven, we were done for the day and following the truck on its way back to the warehouse.

The entire shift ran just over ten hours and that was with working through lunch. I was right — the driver got lazier about checking his mirrors, but it didn't do us much good when there were only a few stops left to make.

I drove by the warehouse parking lot and turned onto the next street. Everyone in the car was quiet. An entire day crammed into a Volkswagen sedan had worn everyone out. I found a Swiss Chalet and pulled into the lot. We needed to talk and I needed to eat. Rick limped more than he had earlier in the morning as he hustled across the lot. He made it to the door ahead of me while Ruby trailed far enough behind for us to have to wait for half a minute at the door for her to catch up. We were seated immediately and after we all had ordered drinks, Rick opened his mouth.

"I don't see what we need this guy for, Ma."

"Rick, please, not now," Ruby said. The old woman looked worn out. She had only been able to eat and drink what she picked up while she surveilled the guards; it was mostly candy bars and bottled water.

"No, I mean it. Why should we cut this guy in for something we can do ourselves? It's my job. I found it and I can do it. We don't need him."

Rick had enough sense to shut his mouth when the waitress came back with our drinks. The teenage girl gave Ruby a coffee, me a tea, and Rick a beer and a shot.

"Are you ready to order?"

"No, we still need a few minutes," Ruby said.

"Okay, just wave when you're ready."

Ruby thanked the girl and Rick downed his shot. He slapped the shot glass down on the table and took a swig of beer.

"Me and Franky could do this no problem. He's already signed on. We smash the truck, take the money, and we're off."

"Sounds like a plan," I said, putting the tea bag into the hot water. "If you need any extra help maybe you should ask the people at the next table. They heard everything you just screamed, so they're already up to speed."

Rick lowered his voice and leaned towards the centre of the table. "Fuck you, asshole. I don't care what my mom told you, this is my job and I'm not cutting you in so I can hear you talk like an asshole while we knock over that truck."

"Not the deal," I said. "I'm not doing the job with you. Never was."

"If you're not doing the job, then why are you here? You owe my mom a favour or something?"

"Think of me as a consultant, Rick. I'm getting paid to plan."

"So what, she tell you you're getting a cut of the score or something? 'Cause I don't think so."

I poured the tea and added milk from one of the tiny containers on the table. I stirred with the watermarked spoon, sipped the tea, and looked at Ruby.

"I am going to sign the house over to Wilson. He will get it when I die."

"No fucking way!" Rick yelled. "The house? That should be mine. What the fuck, Mom?"

The waitress came back to the table looking nervous.

Rick saw her coming and snapped at her. "We're still not ready."

"Oh, uh, right. I just came to tell you that you can't yell like that in here. This is a family restaurant."

"Fuck you," Rick said.

The girl welled up and hurried from the table. I got up, threw down a twenty, and said, "Let's go."

"No way. I'm starving," Rick said.

"If she calls the cops, you won't eat until a lot later."

I walked towards the door and heard Ruby say, "Let's go," to her son.

I debated leaving Ruby and her idiot kid in the parking lot, but that wouldn't get me what I wanted. I needed the house more than I needed peace and quiet. Being able to slip straight into a clean house was an opportunity that wouldn't come around again. I would use the time Ruby had left to construct a new alias. It would take time, and money, for me to get in touch with the kind of people who could make something like that happen. They would help me build an identity on paper that would allow me to live in plain sight. When the old con finally died, I would have identification, credit cards, and a passport in a new name. The second life was necessary to survive. Houses required taxes and bills to be paid, and for that to happen there needed to be a citizen opening his wallet.

"Where to now?" Rick said when he got into the car. "My fuckin' leg is killing me, so there better be no walking."

"I'm taking you home."

"Cool, you're a fucking psycho and a drag."

"I thought we had a deal," Ruby said from the back seat.

"We do," I said. "But my half can wait until tomorrow."

"Are we still on this? Ma, I told you there's no way

this asshole is getting that house. I live in a one-bedroom apartment. I need that place. I don't mean that I want you to die, but come on. What about me?"

There's a spot three inches from the point of the chin that boxers call the magic button. The spot is a hard target to hit because it's on the jawline and therefore is really only about an inch in diameter. The spot isn't magic; there's nothing but pure science at work. Impact at the right point along the jaw reverberates through the skull and shakes the brain with a high degree of force. The grey matter bounces off the hard calcium cage it sits in and causes an instant knockout. It was this one-inch-in-diameter spot that my elbow connected with. The distance between my elbow and Rick's face was small. My hand was on the keys in the ignition so it was two feet at most. It was the pivoting of my hips that gave the elbow enough force to put Rick to sleep. The impact came up from under him and he didn't see it coming. He just crashed back into the headrest and then forward into the dashboard.

"Rick!" Ruby yelled. She climbed over the seat and pulled her boy back into a sitting position. She stroked his face while she looked for any signs of damage. "You didn't have to hit him."

"He had it coming."

"He's just a boy."

"You hear yourself? He's in his twenties. He's a big boy who got himself in serious trouble with some boys who are much bigger. Now, I'm going to take you home. Tomorrow, I'll meet you and Rick at your place. I'll give you a rundown of the job. I see a way to do it, but that's all it is. A way. With the help you have access to, I don't recommend being anywhere near three armed guards, but that's your call."

"What about Rick?"

"I'll put him on your couch."

"He'll be mad when he wakes up."

"Do yourself a favour and tell him to do something about it. I won't kill him, but the hospital time might just save him from the revolvers those guards were carrying."

CHAPTER EIGHT

After I dropped Ruby and the Boy Wonder off, I went back to the house. The rent would be due in a few weeks — a fact that made me acutely aware that there hadn't been any real money coming in for a long time. The rent made me think about the job and the money inside the truck. I had been living off savings while I sorted things out with all the people who wanted me dead. The money slowly drained while the list of people just seemed to keep getting bigger. I put a bullet in almost everyone who came looking to do the same to me, but that was only a temporary solution. There would always be another Paolo or Julian or Sergei; it was just the money that would go away. I had to take advantage of the lull in people wanting to see me dead and start earning again. The armoured car job had potential. The number of stops proved what Rick had said he heard. The truck was definitely doing more than its usual load. He said there were ten trucks to be repaired and that this was week six. There were four heavy Friday runs left. With the right manpower and the right plan, the job could work out. But all that would hinge on keeping Rick and his friend Franky away from the action. I had a few ideas on how to do that, but not all of them would pan out. While I mulled the remaining options over, I dialled up Sully's Tavern.

"Sully's." Steve picked up on the second ring.

"Busy tonight?" I asked.

"Usual."

"What's usual, Steve?" Getting information out of my friend was like trying to get a goldfish to roll over.

"I got to the phone in two rings. What does that tell you?"

"Tells me my seat will be free. See you in a bit."

I hung up the phone and took the Volkswagen over to Sully's. I spent a few hours drinking Coke on a bar stool and talking with Steve while the regulars sat nursing drinks and watching the hockey game. The little bartender was wearing his usual clothes — a white V-neck T-shirt and a pair of khakis. He had a rag over his shoulder and a mop of hair on his head. The hair hung down to his chin and made him look like a skinny sheepdog. I knew Steve better than most and I was always happy to see the shag in front of his eyes. Steve's hair was like a violence barometer. When he pulled it up, someone was about to get hurt or worse. Steve had two settings — normal and homicidal. His wife, Sandra, was like a living, breathing anti-psychotic. When she was around, Steve was in check. Take Sandra out of the equation, or put her in danger, and the little bartender's lizard brain took over. Most people wrote off Steve on account of his size, but the pile of people he put down would go way over anyone's head. He didn't feel pain the way others did and he never got tired. I had seen the carnage he was capable of more than once, and it made me glad every time I walked in and saw his eyes hidden under his hair. The bartender was my only real friend and he had no illusions about what I was. We spoke openly about the job and he put his two cents in whether I liked it or not.

"You haven't done a proper job in a while. Might be time to come out of retirement, or sabbatical, or whatever it is you're on."

"I could use the money," I said.

"I doubt you're broke, but you will be sometime." It was weird how Steve could almost read my thoughts. "Plus, you're paying rent for the first time in a while. That will eat at your savings quicker than you think."

"The house won't be an issue anymore," I said.

Steve laughed. "She's a fucking con. Don't go thinking because you and her go way back that she'll deal straight with you. She's been crooked so long she doesn't know how to be on the level."

I nodded.

"You ever figure out what put the cops on you?"

I thought about the two cops who had recently died because of me. A crooked cop had thought he could string me along like bait for something better to bite at. He had no idea that his partner was in the pocket of a Russian mobster. Both the cop and his partner, along with a Russian mob boss and one of his lieutenants, ended up chum after a shootout that I thought no one could link me to — until my front door came down. "That cop Morrison was smarter than he looked. I'm guessing he had a line on me and the torch got passed to another cop after he went down."

"Cop with a vendetta. Perfect."

"Can't all be successful bartenders," I said.

"You think crooked cops are trouble. Try living with a pregnant wife. Cops just found your front door. I'm sleeping with the enemy."

As though she could hear him talking about her, Sandra emerged from the back room. She said hi to me and then leaned over the bar to give me a kiss on the cheek. Sandra rubbed Steve's back and what little I could see of his cheeks went pink. The most violent man I knew looked human and completely harmless and it made me feel good. I tried to be like that once — regular, connected — but I couldn't do it. The way I felt following the armoured car all day backed up what I already knew. Following the truck felt good; it felt right. My mind was focussed and I was calm, really calm, for the first time in a long while. I couldn't kid myself anymore — I wanted to get back to work.

"Sorry to hear about your place," Sandra said. "How did it happen?"

I went through what I thought had gone down with Sandra and talked with her some more about my housing situation. The talk turned into a conversation that lasted a few hours.

I went home from the bar late, but happy with what I had accomplished. I had gotten done what I had planned to take care of before I met with Ruby and Rick the next day without getting off the bar stool. With my schedule clear, I had nothing left to think about but the job. I sat on the living room floor, in the corner beside the front window. I had no blinds, so the streetlight bled in. I watched the strobes of passing cars and listened to the sound of the vehicles passing. The sounds were rhythmic, like man-made waves, and as I listened I slowed my breathing. This wasn't something that my uncle had taught me. I had read about meditation in some old books I found at a garage sale and taught myself the techniques. In the pile of books, I also found a dog-eared book written by a samurai. The samurai had fought over sixty duels in his lifetime and was never defeated. I learned another practice from the samurai's words. The ancient warrior described visualizing death in every possible form over and over so that the inherent fear of dying lost its power. The goal was to become so familiar with death that it was no longer another opponent to fight against, but rather something that travelled with you everywhere. I practised the samurai's lessons until death lost its venom. The old swordsman had developed something valuable and I expanded the teaching to the jobs I worked. Instead of visualizing death, I visualized each job going wrong in every possible way.

Over the years, I had learned to relax and spend hours running through what needed to be done in my mind. I ran through scenario after scenario, letting my mind devise every kind of interruption and complication. I sat for hours on the floor, the buzz of traffic barely noticeable, as I repeated the job again and again. I died a hundred times, and wore steel bracelets a hundred more, until my brain found a way through the minefield and I walked away with the money inside the armoured truck.

CHAPTER NINE

spent the next morning working out. Living in the city meant I had access to numerous facilities that were stocked with the most current fitness technology, but I ignored the new gyms and found an old place that catered to power-lifters and athletes instead of spandex-wearing yuppies with iPods attached to their arms. The gym had a large workout area stocked with nothing but metal. There were no moving parts or electronics, just simple machines with levers and pulleys and plenty of iron to move.

I walked to the rack of kettlebells being ignored by the rest of the gym members and picked up an eighty-pound weight. Kettlebells were an old Russian design and they were equal parts torture device and workout equipment. The weight looked simple enough: an eighty-pound sphere attached to a thick handle. I picked up the kettlebell with my right hand and cleaned it to my shoulder. I then pressed the kettlebell into the air. I repeated the motion ten times and then switched hands and did the whole thing over again. After four sets, I moved to swings and then rows, forcing myself to push the weight faster and harder. By the time I started Turkish get-ups, I was drenched. The kettle-bell was more than just a weight to move, it was an aerobic activity. Every muscle in my body was run down and beat up by the Russian device, but I kept it moving, knowing I would come away stronger and faster.

After the workout, I got a tea and a doughnut, and drove the same route I had followed the armoured car through the day before. The plan forming in my head would get the money out of the truck and us away, but there were still variables that had to be dealt with. The job was like a jigsaw puzzle. I had all of the pieces, but I still needed to fit them together. I went into each store the guards had dragged the money into and scouted the ATMs, the cameras, the exits, and the parking lots. It took a couple of hours to get through the whole route — it was much faster when I didn't have to wait for two guys to load an ATM with cash. I broke for lunch at a Thai restaurant and then revisited the first four stops. If you're going to hit a truck double full of money, it's best to hit it while it's still double full. I cased each of the locations in widening circles looking for the corners of my puzzle. It was the first stop that had everything: the most money, the emptiest lot, and — most important — a way out.

I stopped at an Internet café that offered printing for five cents a page and then made a run for some Middle Eastern takeout before driving over to Ruby's place. On the way, I made a quick stop and picked up an envelope that was waiting for me. I was at Ruby's by eight. I knocked on the door and it was answered by Ruby.

"Hey, Ruby," I said.

She looked pale. Her wig was up under a bandana and she wore a purple sweatshirt and grey sweatpants that were both way too big. On her feet were worn-out slippers.

MIKE KNOWLES

"Hey, Wilson. It's not really a good time."

I was about to say something when I heard Rick say, "Is that him? Oh, that motherfucker is dead now. Dead!"

I could hear plates being shoved aside, a chair being shoved back, and then loud footsteps. There was more than one person.

Rick and another twenty-something barged into the hallway. Rick had on cargo pants and a Green Lantern T-shirt. His friend wore a LeBron James jersey and black cargo pants over unlaced Timberlands; on his head, he wore a black ballcap turned sideways. He had a beard that was maybe four days old. Rick was six feet tall with the kind of muscle a high-school quarterback would carry; his friend was a hell of a lot bigger. He wore nothing under the jersey and I saw thick veins running like pipelines down his arms.

Rick charged up to his mother's back; the other guy kept a bit of distance. "Surprised you'd show your face after you sucker-punched me."

"It was no sucker punch," I said.

"What?"

"There's hit and not hit. You got hit. How I hit you doesn't matter. Same as dead and alive. There's no degree of either. You're either dead or you're alive."

"What the hell are you talking about?" Rick wanted to know.

"I'm just trying to explain that sucker punch is just a term invented by people who were too embarrassed to admit that they were members of the got hit club."

"And I'm in that club?"

"Yep."

"Franky, let's teach this motherfucker the club's secret handshake."

Franky didn't look like he really wanted to fight, but he

balled his fists and stepped forward anyway. Rick started to move around Ruby, but she lifted her arms to hold him back.

"I won't have this in my house. I invited him in and I say we're going to let him in so we can hear what he has to say."

"The hell we are," Rick said. "Me and Franky are going to fuck him up."

Rick bear-hugged his mom and turned her around so that she was out of the way.

"Careful, man," Franky said.

"Shut up, Franky. I barely touched her," Rick fired back.

Franky had nothing else to say; neither did Rick after he turned around and saw the Glock.

"There's two categories of shot too. Shot and not shot. Which category are you going to be in, Rick?"

"Not shot," Rick said.

"Franky?"

"Nnn . . . not shot," he said. He put his hands in the air and took a step back towards the kitchen.

"Put the gun away," Ruby said.

The gun stayed where it was.

"Did you hear what I said? I remember you with pimples, boy, so don't you think I'm going to let you in here waving a gun. Rick is just mad. He has every right to be."

"Damn straight," Rick said.

Ruby whirled on him. "But he's going to get over it because there are more important things to deal with than who punched who. Now, everybody in the kitchen."

The two in front of me turned around and went back the way they came. I let the gun down and put it away.

"Goddamn men and their testosterone bullshit," Ruby said. "Everything has to be about chest beating. You should know better."

"Stop telling me what I should know. You're his mother, not mine. And you came to me for help, not the other way around."

"Fine," she said. "Will you come into the kitchen? Pretty please with sugar on top."

"Was that so hard?" I said.

"Get the fuck in there, Wilson." She had an ice-cold look on her face.

"Yes, ma'am," I said. I hustled into the kitchen ahead of the old woman and her anger.

The kitchen had cheap cabinets with white paint peeling off the lower doors. The stove and fridge were butter yellow and both looked old enough to have been prototypes. The table was round and looked as if it would provide tight seating for four. Rick and Franky sat opposite each other, leaving two seats. My choices were either being wedged against the wall, or sitting with my back exposed to the hallway. I hated to have the open hallway at my back, but being shoved against the wall with no room to manoeuvre seemed worse. I took the seat closer to the hall and Rick said, "That's my mother's seat. You get the other one."

I stayed put. Ruby said, "What now?" as she came in behind me.

"He's in your chair, Ma. Tell him to get out. It's your house. Or is that it? You think you own the place already? You're some guy taking a lady's house from her while she's sick. I don't know how you sleep at night. But maybe scumbags like you don't have any trouble closing their eyes."

"It's okay," Ruby said. "I'll sit over there. I don't mind. Really, I don't."

"But I do, Ma."

"It will be his house soon enough. Let him sit where he wants."

Rick waved his hand. "Whatever, what the fuck ever. Fine, go ahead, asshole, earn your house."

I put the envelope on the table and slid out the papers inside. "This job is like any other transaction. I'm going to need the money up front."

"Money up front?" Rick said. "We haven't done the job yet, so how can there be money up front?"

"He wants the house now," Ruby said.

"You're going to kick my mother, sick with cancer, out of her house. No way! No goddamn way!"

"I'm not going to kick her out. She can live here for the rest of her days, however many that may be, but the house won't be in her name." I pushed the paperwork across the table to Ruby. At the bar the night before, I had told Sandra about the deal I had with Ruby and I mentioned that I needed to find the right kind of real estate agent — someone who would bend the law for a fee. Sandra told me that her cousin was an agent and that he could probably get us where we needed to go. Sandra's cousin passed us off to a real estate lawyer. The guy was a Serbian who was known, in some small circles, to do some shady work for other immigrants. I used the phone at the bar to call the lawyer's cell. He uh-hunh'ed his way through my bullshit story about wanting to avoid all of the red tape and taxes after my grandma died. He knew I was spinning bullshit and he didn't care. He told me a price that was anything but bullshit, and I agreed. I stopped at his office before I went to Ruby's and everything I asked for was ready.

"Fill in your name and all of your info. Sign and initial where indicated and you will have added me to the deed of your house."

"This wasn't part of the deal. It was supposed to be after I died, Wilson."

"Something you said yesterday got me thinking. You

said that you would do anything for your kids. You'd pay any price, go to any length. If the job went south —" I put a lot of emphasis on "if" because it wasn't the word I wanted to use. "You'd sell this place in a heartbeat to get him lawyered up right. You'd cross me and I know it. These papers make sure that we'll all stay friends no matter what."

"The hell it does. Don't sign it, Ma. I got everything figured."

"Rick's right," Franky said.

"Tell me what you got figured, Rick."

"No way."

"I'll tell you what. You tell me what you got up your sleeve, and if your mom can agree that it is a solid plan, I'll get up and leave. Your mom keeps the house and you do the job yourself."

"You'll just try and rob the truck before us."

"It doesn't work that way, Rick. I never wanted this job. I signed on for the house. You want it back, just show me I'm not needed."

"Fine, we stop the truck with two vans. Y'know, pull up in front and behind. Franky puts explosives on the back door while I cover the front with a rifle. An M4 like in *Call of Duty*. I see one of the guys up front move and I'll stitch them up with the gun so that the other will know better than to fuck with me. Franky blows the door and he pulls out the guard in back. He brings the guy out in front of the truck and we make the other two get out or else we'll blow his brains out. They'll do it. They're just guys making a shitty salary; they don't want to die for the cash. I cover the guards while Franky backs the van up bumper to bumper with the truck. He loads the van and then swings around to pick me up. I shoot out the truck tires and we're gone in under three minutes." Rick slapped the table in triumph. "Now get the fuck out and take your papers with you."

I leaned back and sighed. Ruby looked disappointed; it was like she asked him what two plus two was and he said ten. It took a long time for her to look across the table and meet my eyes. When she did, I said, "You want to tell him, or should I?"

"Tell me what? Tell him to get the fuck out. My plan is legit."

Ruby shook her head at me.

"Let's start from the top. Where are you going to get two vans?"

"Steal them."

"You know how?"

"I can learn. It's on the Internet."

"Fine, let's say you do. Where are you going to pull this daring daylight heist? In the street? In the parking lot? What are you going to do about witnesses? People see a robbery they're going to call the cops or tape you with their phones."

"We find a quiet spot," Rick said.

"You did the route with me yesterday. You see any quiet spots?"

"Like I said, we'll find one."

"Fine," I said. "Let's say you do find a quiet spot. Where are the explosives going to come from?"

Franky opened his mouth to get this one. "Ho —"

"Don't you dare say Home Depot. They don't sell explosives, but let's say you did manage to find them and to get around the mess of red tape surrounding the sale and distribution of explosives. How much would you use?"

"How much?" There was less bravado in Rick's voice now.

"Too little and those big heavy doors won't move. Too

much and you blow up the money, not to mention kill the guard back there."

"Who cares about the guard? They're just junior pigs in training."

"Killing a guard ups the ante. It's not just a robbery after that. You kill a man and you'll get a whole new level of attention from the cops. But let's say, for the sake of argument, that you get the explosives just right. Where do you get the M4 to aim at the bank guards?"

"I know a guy."

"This guy ever tell you specifically that he has assault rifles, or did you just assume that because he could get his hands on a piece that a machine gun would be no problem?"

Rick didn't answer.

"Let's say he does have the guns. Where will you come up with the couple grand you'll need to buy them?"

Rick looked out the window instead of at me.

I kept going. "You ever fired an assault rifle?"

"No," Rick sounded petulant.

"But you're sure you could fire through bulletproof glass and hit one of the guards if you had to."

"I could fuckin' do it, man."

"No, all you can do is watch television. What happened, you watch *Heat* and think if De Niro can do it, you can too?"

Rick gave the window some more of his attention.

"Yeah, I saw that movie too, Rick. Tell me, how many guys did De Niro have in his crew? There was Val Kilmer, the scary Mexican, the guy from the rehab show who dated the madam, and another guy they took on for the job because four wasn't enough. That's five guys on a job you thought you could streamline down to two. I could see that. There was a lot of wasted manpower there. Was the mistake because of bad planning on De Niro's part, or was it the fact that it was a fucking movie?"

No one would look at me now. We all sat in silence until Ruby decided to move. She took the pen out of the envelope I brought and started going through the papers. She filled in her information and signed and initialled everything. When she slid the document back to me, I said, "My guy will make all of this legal. The house is yours until you don't need it anymore."

"Fine," Ruby said in a small voice. "Just tell me your plan."

I put the papers back in the envelope and got started. "First of all, it's not a two-man job. The movies got it right with five people. The van wasn't a bad idea either." Rick looked at me with a smug I-told-you-so look on his face. "Just one van," I said, "not two. What you won't need is explosives. The cost, time it takes to find the materials, and training we'd need make them a bad idea."

Rick was back to looking sullen.

"Let's start with the where. I ran the route again yesterday and it makes the most sense to hit the truck at the first stop. The early time of day means fewer potential witnesses and more money in the truck."

"Makes sense," Rick said. Franky and Ruby nodded.

"I'm glad you think so. If your intel is correct, you have four Fridays left to pull the job. You'll need at least two weeks to get ready."

"Two weeks?"

"The first thing you need," I said, ignoring Rick, "is a way into the truck. The armoured car is exactly what it sounds like — armoured. Getting at the money won't be easy. The movements of the guards are professional and practised. The back door is never open longer than thirty seconds, and the guard riding shotgun spends most of

MIKE KNOWLES

that time with his hand on the butt of his gun. The driver also never leaves the cab, and he checks his mirrors constantly. A straight stickup would fall apart fast. The driver would be on the radio before we even got near the money. Smashing the truck and blowing it open, like the movie, won't work either. A good demo man could only estimate the amount of explosives to use, and when paper money is inside even a small miscalculation can mean a whole lot of barbecued cash."

"No plan so far," Rick said.

"I'm trying to make you understand. The truck is the problem. Its design makes it almost impossible to crack."

"So what do we do?" Ruby asked.

"You go after something else," I said. "Something softer and easier to break. The guard driving the rig has a cell phone on. He took several calls when the other two were delivering the money. Having the phone on and using it on duty is probably a no-no, but the guy up front is so bored sitting there by himself that he risks it. The phone is our way in. We use that to force the driver to do what we need him to do. That is the chink in the armour."

"Watch it with the chink shit," Rick said.

"It's an expression," Ruby said.

"I know, Ma. I was kiddin'," Rick lied. "So how do we use the phone to get in? We just call him up and ask him nicely to get out with his hands in the air?"

"That's why you need two weeks. You need the time to get the right gear and to figure out where the driver is weak. On Monday, you get your mother to follow the driver home. It won't take her more than a few days to figure out who he's calling. If I were going to bet, I'd say he's calling a wife or girlfriend. Ruby finds whoever it is and then she has a week to observe them. She needs to insert herself in the person's life so that on the following Friday, she can get you into their house after the driver leaves for work."

"Are we going to ransom her for the truck?" Franky asked.

I shook my head. "You're going to bolt her into the back of a van and pull up in front of the armoured car right after the other two guards go in. You open the back doors and let the driver see his wife, girlfriend, mother, or whatever. You signal for the driver to call her phone and when he does, you get him to open the door. The driver gets pulled into the van while one of your guys gets behind the wheel of the truck."

Rick was nodding his head. "And just like that, the money is ours."

"No, you just have the truck and a seven-minute window. Seven minutes was their average time inside; you could probably push it to ten or twelve minutes if Ruby makes sure that she gets to the ATM first."

"I thought she was getting us into the wife's place," Franky said.

"That was when the driver left for work. He still has to go to the warehouse, check the truck, load up, and whatever else they do. Ruby should have plenty of time to get to the grocery store ahead of the armoured car."

Ruby nodded in agreement.

"Ruby should be able to get you twelve minutes with the truck. Once that time is up, you'll be driving a cop magnet. The truck will be outfitted with GPS and every single squad car in the city will be on the lookout once the other guards radio in a problem. You need to get everything out of the truck before all hell breaks loose."

I pulled a folded printout from the Internet café from my pocket and opened it up on the table.

"What's this?" Rick asked.

"Directions. Less than a click away from the grocery store, there's an abandoned gas station. The service bays are empty and wide enough to accommodate an armoured car. You get the doors unlocked ahead of time and drive the truck in. You'll have burned a minute and a half getting there, leaving you just over ten minutes to off-load the money into the van. The driver and his leverage get cuffed to the truck and you drive the van out."

I pulled another piece of paper from my pocket, unfolded it, and slid it across the table. "This is a building for lease about ten kilometres from the job. The building used to be a school, but it hasn't been in use for years. The property is on a big lot and the trees around the school are all overgrown. The van will be completely out of sight parked out back. The school is a good place to count the money and divvy it up. You'll pack some food and sleeping bags there and spend the night."

"Spend the night? What the fuck for?" Rick wanted to know.

"Once word gets out about the truck, the whole city will be on alert. They'll be expecting you to run, and they'll act accordingly — meaning roadblocks. The most dangerous place to be will be on the road, so you need to be off it. The next day, the cops will have relaxed the citywide search because they'll think you got out before they could clamp everything down. The investigation will be on the shoulders of major crimes division, and they won't be watching the roads — they'll be too busy interviewing people. That's when you load up your cars, firebomb the van, and go your separate ways."

Rick looked at the two maps and chewed his lower lip. "There's a lot to do. Tons to get ready."

"Like I said, it's a five-man job."

"Five cuts up the pie more than I want."

"Screwing it up will get you nothing," I said.

"Could we use four?" Ruby asked.

"Four could work, but everything would have to run tight. My recommendation, right now you got one pro and two amateurs — get some decent help if you want to pull this off."

I picked up the real estate paperwork and nodded my goodbye to the people at the table. No one said goodbye to me as I left the kitchen. I walked out the front door and got halfway to my car before Ruby got a hold of my arm.

"Wait."

"Deal's done, Ruby. I did my part."

"New deal, Wilson. You help us with the job."

I looked hard at the little woman. She had already started shivering in the night air and her grip on my arm spasmed. "The plan is good, but your boy doesn't have it in him to run something like this."

"That's why we need you. I can make him listen. He'll do what you tell him."

"You know he won't. He's a dumb fucking kid with more pride than brains."

"You were a dumb kid once."

"That was a long time ago, and I was never like him."

"That was because you had your uncle to help you."

I saw where she was going with this. It felt just like when you notice that a bird is flying over your head and you realize that you don't have time to move before the shit lands on your skull. "It was nothing like that. I asked him to teach me to be like him. I signed on for it and I did every goddamn thing he said without question. Rick is an ungrateful little shit who isn't satisfied with going down with the ship alone. Even now he's more concerned with divvying up the money than with walking away clean. Getting away is everything. The score is second."

"Bring in someone else. Someone you can trust," Ruby said.

"Your boy said he didn't want a five-way pay out."

"He can have my share. That way there's no problem. He gets his money, you get three pros. Plus the house and a cut of the money. We'll give Rick and Franky small jobs, and I promise to keep Rick in line. Please, Wilson, your family needs you."

I didn't feel any tugs on my heartstrings for Rick or Ruby. They weren't my family and I owed them nothing. Something else was pulsating below the surface. Planning the job had woken something inside me. All of a sudden, it felt like I was waking from a coma and flexing muscles that had lain dormant for too long. I wanted to do the job. I saw every angle and knew I could pull it off. With Ruby, and someone else reliable, it would be a profitable ten minutes' work.

I gave it a few more seconds of unnecessary thought before I said, "Alright." Ruby could think she won me over with her pleas about family if she wanted. I wasn't going to correct her, just like I wasn't going to give her back the deed to her place or make sure that she got a cut of the money.

I spoke with Ruby for a few more minutes and then got in the car. I told her I would pick up some help for the job and then get in touch with her about our next move. Ruby didn't look cold anymore. She had stopped shivering and she wore the happiest smile I had ever seen.

hadn't been Ruby's only choice for the job. I had heard that she was asking about a few other names besides mine when she was cruising the bars late at night. One of the people she asked about was Dave Book. D.B. was a member of the Forty Thieves — a biker gang that was big in Southern Ontario. D.B. had earned his patch at sixteen. He rode without a licence on a stolen bike and kicked the shit out of anyone who thought he should be different. He was a hulk of a man with short blond hair and a tightly trimmed goatee. Now forty-seven, he was out of jail and second in command of the Thieves. Second in command meant D.B. was the one who got his hands dirty. The boss didn't kill anyone, or supervise drug shipments — that was all left to D.B.

It being Sunday, I knew where D.B. would be. He would start the day at the gym before going to play a few games of bocce ball. Somewhere along the line, the giant biker had learned that he had a talent for the game. He was now obsessed and would play until the snow blanketed the ground. His court was a small field downtown where he played with a bunch of retirees, none of whom looked to have ever ridden a Harley in their lives.

I found D.B. with three other men at the court. The old men were bundled in heavy coats, scarves, and hats. D.B. was in jeans and a T-shirt. His massive arms were covered in ink and laced with veins. I saw his leather jacket in a heap beside two of the old men who were sitting on a bench watching the game. I took a seat on the sidelines and watched as D.B. waited for his turn. The ball in his giant hands looked like a tennis ball compared to the one the senior beside him was clutching in his veined paws. The jack was almost a hundred feet away from where the two men stood. The old man tossed his bocce ball underhand and it skipped over the frozen ground and landed within feet of the jack. The old man's ball was white and it was closest to the marker, leaving D.B.'s two black balls behind it and therefore worthless.

"Good toss, Herb. Good toss," D.B. said.

"Thanks, D.B." Herb clapped the big man on the shoulder and slowly walked his bent body over to his friends on the bench. The old man was completely at ease with the giant biker.

"Well, folks, Herb is inside, so I guess it's my turn to make him cry."

"Dream on," Herb yelled from his seat.

"Old man, I must be asleep because —" D.B. lobbed the ball high, using a completely different style than the old man. Instead of bouncing down the court, D.B.'s ball crashed down on top of the old man's ball. Herb's ball skittered sideways like it had been struck by the gods above. D.B.'s ball rolled some, but it stayed within three feet of the jack. "Because I just sent you outside."

Herb got up and called D.B. a thug. The biker laughed

and I smiled. I had seen him break bones for less. D.B. marked three points for the round and the men started another. The big biker saw me when he went to collect his balls and I raised my cup. He waved and sent the balls back to the line. The game went on for another twenty minutes. Herb racked up a good number of points and D.B. managed to win only by two. The November morning air was cold and it was only the tea and watch cap that kept me from shivering. I had no idea how D.B. could play in just a T-shirt. Once the game was over, D.B. saw the three men off. It was a hell of a sight watching the biker gently help one of the old men into the back seat of the light blue Grand Marquis they all came in. I walked onto the court feeling the air blowing against my face. I caught sight of a single snowflake and watched as it flew out of sight. I opened D.B.'s case and picked up one of the balls the biker had used. The polished black ball weighed around two pounds. I thought about the high arcing shots the biker had thrown, and the ease with which he did it, and figured there was no way in hell I could match his distance or accuracy.

The white jack left D.B.'s hand, landed at the end of the court, and rolled to a stop. "Take the first shot," D.B. said.

"I haven't played in years. Not since the last time you beat me."

"It was a shutout, if I recall."

D.B. was right about the score. I remembered it because it was a huge loss and the last time I played. The fact that D.B. remembered the score, considering the countless games he must have played since, made me smile. It was easy to look at D.B. and write him off as a meathead. But he was no idiot; D.B. had one of the sharpest minds I had ever come across. It was probably why he had turned down Ruby.

NEVER PLAY ANOTHER MAN'S GAME

"Heard you skipped town," he said.

"I did. Had some problems with the Italians and the Russians."

"Pussies," D.B. said. He was one of the few people who could say that about the mobs without a hint of bullshit. D.B. wasn't afraid of anyone or anything, not even a war with those ruthless gangsters. I doubted he would have run if he had been in my place. He would have fought, and probably died, but he would have surely taken more of the other side with him. The only time I had ever seen D.B. lose a fight was when he took on Steve. The little bartender climbed up D.B.'s body like it was a redwood and chopped him down. The story was legendary for those who saw it because it was never spoken of again. No one wanted to be the one who gossiped about D.B. losing a fight.

"Trouble's over and now it's back to work. You looking for a job, or are the Thieves paying you so well that you don't need to moonlight anymore?"

"You know bikers don't do it for the paycheque. We get paid in pussy and beer more often than in cash. The Thieves do keep me busy, though. I don't get to do side jobs often anymore."

"I heard you turned down Ruby."

"That's what you're here about? Shit, Wilson, I didn't think you were that hard up for cash. I'm disappointed, bro. I thought you had more sense than that."

"Did she tell you about the job?"

"She didn't have to. Her and that kid of hers showed up and tried to get me on the payroll."

"So you met Rick?"

D.B. nodded. "If Ruby hadn't been standing there, looking so sick, I would have knocked his teeth in."

"I hit him with a car," I said.

D.B. laughed. "Same old Wilson. So if you met the kid,

why the hell would you sign on for the job?"

"Ain't his job anymore — it's mine," I said.

"That changes things."

"You blowing off Ruby is what changed things. She realized no one would sign on for the job, so she hired me to plan it for her. She figured if she had the right plan, the kid could run the job himself."

D.B. laughed. "It's just that simple. Like putting together something from IKEA. She ask you to draw pictures for the kid in case things get complicated?"

"The kid's a retard, no argument, but he stumbled onto an armoured car driving around with two shifts' worth of money. The score is right and the job can be done if the crew is right too."

"The kid still involved?"

I nodded.

"Then how can the crew ever be right? He'll fuck it up for sure."

"If we work with Ruby, that's three pros. You know people have done plenty of jobs with a couple of professionals and a civilian insider. Most of the bigger scores need one."

"But not all the civilians want to come along for the ride. The smart ones are happy to sit back and let us do the heavy lifting while they wait for their cut."

"No argument, but the score is worth the risk. If it's done right, we all go home with a hell of a lot of shekels in our pockets."

"Tell me the plan," D.B. said.

He listened to what I had to say with a bocce ball in his hand. As I spoke he gently tossed the ball up in the air over and over again, catching the heavy orb with one hand as though it were a tennis ball. He didn't stop me as I ran through the plan; he just nodded every now and again.

When I finished, he said, "I only see two problems."

"Rick and Franky," I said.

"Yeah, you have them out of the action, but who's to say that they'll stay that way. They fuck up their part and we all go down."

"Show me a job without risk that comes with a pay-day like this. If you're waiting for an offer to knock over an armoured car that doesn't involve risk, you'll look like Herb before it happens."

"Hey, Herb is a solid dude."

"He is, and he's living off a tiny pension wasting his time playing with you in the cold instead of with someone his own age down in Florida. That what you want when you're his age?"

D.B. looked at the jack he had thrown down the court. "If I say no, who's next on your list?"

"Wally."

"He'll say yeah for sure. He's an action junkie. Good at what he does too."

I nodded.

"Why'd you come to me first? You know I already said no."

"Two reasons. You're better than Wally and your connections with the Thieves can get us whatever equipment we need."

"No one ever really loves me for me," D.B. said.

"You in or out, D.B.?"

The huge biker threw his bocce ball onto the field. The ball bounced its way to the end of the court and stopped three inches from the marker. "Tell ya what, bro. We play one round. You beat me and I'm in."

I picked up a ball and aimed at the marker. My ball ended up a foot away from D.B.'s.

"You're going to need to do a hell of a lot better than

that if you want me on the job, bro."

"Just throw, D.B."

"It's your turn again. I'm inside and you, pal, are on the outside. You need to get closer to the jack than me before I have to throw again."

"How do you play in a T-shirt? It's freezing out."

"Coat fucks with my swing, bro. Sometimes you gotta suffer to be great."

It took two more throws before I managed to connect with D.B.'s ball. My shot knocked his farther away and put me inside.

D.B. laughed and bent his knees. His arm drifted back and then came forward in a smooth, powerful swing. His ball landed on top of my last shot and sent the ball out of position with such force that it smashed into the curb on the side of the court and ricocheted back towards me.

"I'm on the inside again, outsider."

My last shot rolled within an inch of the marker and kept going until it stopped a foot away. All of D.B.'s balls were closer to the jack. D.B. laughed at the shot and then said, "When do we meet?"

"I lost, D.B. You're off the hook."

"What, you think I'm going to let a game decide my life? Don't be stupid. We're talking about an armoured car here. You saying it can be got is good enough for me. I'm in, bro."

"What was the point of the game, then?"

"To see if you got any better. You didn't."

I walked over to the fence and said, "Tomorrow night we'll meet in Sully's."

"That little bartender still around?"

I nodded. The fight not heard 'round the world didn't sour D.B. on Steve. Instead, the fight fostered a fondness for the smaller man in D.B. He respected Steve for being able to put him down sort of the same way a father respects his son when he manages to beat him at something.

"Think he's up for round two?"

I looked over at D.B. "Stick to beating old men," I said.

"Don't go away mad. Let's play again."

"Forget it. I knock off trucks, not balls."

"You beat me and I'll give you my share."

I turned around and took off my coat.

t snowed on the day of the job, not enough to make the roads slick — just enough to see wisps of snow slithering over the pavement like snakes made of confetti. I sat in the passenger seat of the van; Franky was driving.

"Breathe," I said.

"I am breathing. It's part of being alive. All aerobic organisms require oxygen to release energy."

"Aerobic organisms? You a college boy, Franky?"

"What? No. I just watch a lot of TV."

"Well, you're panting, Discovery Channel. Take the breaths slow and easy. You need to be able to think. Panting like a dog isn't going to get you there."

"I can hear you from here, Franky," Rick said.

It was strange. Franky was the only one breathing hard. Rick was just as new to this as his partner, but he seemed to have everything together. There was no nervous chatter or stupid bravado; he just sat on the floor behind the front seats holding the AK-47 D.B. had procured from whatever biker source he had. When D.B. delivered the two rifles, he told us to avoid firing them at all costs.

"It'll be sweet if I can sell them back to the guy clean."

D.B. bankrolled the firearms. That meant he would get the money he spent back out of the take before we divvied the rest up. If he wanted to make a little extra selling the guns back, no one was going to argue.

The butt of the second AK was leaning against the door beside me. I watched out through the window as Ruby knocked on the door. The driver's name was Rob. He lived with a wife and kid in a small house in the suburb of Dundas. Every day, Rob left at six thirty. The wife came out an hour later, with the kid, and waited at the curb. The kid got on the bus at seven thirty-five and then the wife went back inside. She was a stay-at-home mom who pulled in a little extra cash selling cosmetics. Ruby used the side business to work her way into the woman's life. She met Rob's wife, Donna, on the street and faked being new to the neighbourhood. Ruby was a con artist by trade and when put in her element, she could move mountains and steal fortunes with nothing more than words. Ruby power-walked by the house every morning, catching Donna waiting with the kid for the bus. She made a small Avon order in the first week and then a large one the following Thursday. She told Donna she would drop off the cash Friday morning when she came by on her usual morning walk, but Ruby was later than usual and the bus came and went before she got to the house. Ruby had to knock on the door to give Donna her big cheque.

Ruby stood on the porch waiting. In her hand, she held an Avon book. To her left, D.B. stood leaning against the side of the house. He was wearing black jeans and a black T-shirt. He had changed jackets, opting for a plain leather coat without any of his usual gang patches. He needlessly wore a pair of black wraparound sunglasses. Who could argue with the logic of a six-and-a-half-foot giant who told you he liked to look the part?

The door opened after a minute and Ruby and Donna engaged in what looked like a bit of friendly banter. Ruby stayed on the porch and convinced Donna to step outside by accidentally dropping her purse. Donna stepped onto the porch to help Ruby pick up her things and I saw the cold hit her all at once. The below-zero air dug into the old sweats she had on and Donna immediately started hugging her body.

The friendly chit-chat went on, probably about the weather, and I saw D.B. move away from the wall. The big man came out from around the side of the house and grabbed Donna from behind while she was in mid-sentence. D.B.'s martial arts training was solid and he put a textbook rear naked choke on the much smaller woman. Her one-hundred-and-thirty-pound frame, much of the weight in her butt, went rigid with fear and then slack with unconsciousness in about ten seconds. D.B. picked the woman up as Ruby stepped into the house. D.B. started down the driveway and before he got to the curb Ruby was back on the porch with another purse in her hands. Rick had the back doors of the van open for D.B. and Donna went into the chair I had spot-welded to the floor. D.B. zip-tied her hands to the chair while I did her feet. I taped her mouth and put a tote bag Ruby had gotten for free from a bulk food store over her head. The fabric bag was loose and there was no way Donna would suffocate under it.

"You get to carry a tote bag while I have to carry the girl. Tell me how that is fair?"

"I thought doing the heavy lifting would be good for your self-esteem. You spend so much time with the elderly, I didn't want you to feel like you weren't a man anymore," I said.

"I love how you're always thinking of me, bro."

I blew D.B. a kiss and closed the doors. Franky started the engine and had the van away from the curb before I was even back in my seat.

"Wilson, what did you mean when you said D.B. hung out with the elderly? He got a fetish or something?" Franky asked as he rolled through a stop sign.

"No names, dummy," Rick said. "And watch the traffic signs. We don't want to get pulled over with Donna here tied up in back."

Rick had gotten the rebuke out before I could. The kid wasn't only cooler than he looked, he was smarter too.

"Sorry . . . uh, dude."

We drove to the grocery store parking lot with D.B. and Ruby trailing behind in a Jeep Wrangler we boosted. By five after eight, we were parked in the far corner of the lot. Donna had woken up and she was making muffled sounds through the tape on her mouth. She had started out in a panic, but when no one spoke to her or touched her, her hysteria reduced to silent terror.

Franky couldn't stop looking at the struggling woman. He had never pulled a job like this before, so a little fear was common. Rick, on the other hand, was as cool as last night's leftovers. He alternated looks at his watch and the entrance and he kept his mouth shut unless he had something important to say. There had been no whining or bullshit behaviour all morning. I was starting to wonder if the kid had more of my uncle's blood in him than I thought.

I nudged Franky to get his attention off the woman when I saw the truck coming into the lot.

I looked over at the black Jeep just in time to see Ruby getting out. She had changed outfits and was now dressed in a windbreaker and tapered cotton pants. The pants were a light blue stretchy fabric that ended just above the ankles. Ruby's white socks introduced even whiter orthopaedic running shoes. She looked ten years older than she was, especially with the grey wig I had found for her. She pushed a metal cart that she had brought with her into the store. She was just another senior citizen going into the store for a little early morning shopping. And like most seniors, Ruby would be absolutely shit at using an ATM.

Ruby walked into the store just as the guard riding shotgun stepped out of the cab. The guard opened the back door, pulled the cash out, and waited for the guard in back to get onto the pavement. I couldn't be sure that the driver up front would have keys for the back of the truck so it was up to Ruby to pick them off the guard. I wasn't worried about her end; there was a better chance of lightning striking me than of Ruby screwing up a simple pick.

The guards moved like they always did and as soon as they were inside, I tapped Franky on the shoulder. We all pulled ski masks on and Franky gunned the engine. The van bucked ahead and Donna screamed as loud as she could under the tape. I clicked my watch as we moved across the lot and I heard a beep from behind me that came from Rick starting his own stopwatch. Rick Junior was picking things up fast.

The van pulled to the curb in front of the armoured truck. Franky threw it in reverse and pulled within six feet of the truck. Rick opened the rear doors and pulled the tote bag off Donna's face while I climbed into the rear of the van. He held up the sign we made the night before next to Donna's face; I put a gun to her head. The armoured car guard's face was a mix of confusion and horror as he read the sign and realized its implications.

CALL YOUR WIFE'S CELL NOW! NO RADIO OR SHE DIES!

It took ten seconds for the phone in my hand to ring. I

NEVER PLAY ANOTHER MAN'S GAME

pressed talk and heard the driver.

"You son of a bitch!"

I ignored the curse and laid out the deal. "Rob, put your right hand on the windshield and keep the phone to your ear with the left or we shoot her in the knee."

Rick heard me and put the sign down. He picked up the AK and pointed it at Donna's leg. The movement was smooth and the gun didn't waver. He pressed the muzzle against her knee and looked at the driver. I wasn't worried about anyone seeing us — the lot was still pretty empty and we had pulled back close enough for the open van doors to block the view of anyone who might drive by. The heavy tinting D.B. had applied to the van windows made the ski mask on Franky impossible to see up front. The driver, Rob, had a lone front-row seat for our show. He nodded to us, switched the phone to the other hand, and then put a shaky right hand against the windshield.

"Good," I said. "Now, hold the phone against your shoulder and open the door with your left. Then, put your other hand against the windshield."

"No fucking way," he said.

"Shoot her in the knee," I said to Rick.

Donna heard the command. She screamed under the tape and bucked in her chair, but the zip ties held her in place. Rick took a hand off the AK and used it to shield his eyes so that the contents of her knee wouldn't blind him when they splashed all over the van. I had shown Rick the exact stance when we prepped the job. It was a bad way to stand in terms of accuracy — the gun would jump when he pulled the trigger and the one-handed grip might mean a miss, but I didn't really want him to shoot Donna. One shot in the parking lot would put the whole job out the window. If the guards didn't hear it, a pedestrian would and they'd run for cover inside the store. After that, there would be nothing to do but run. The threat of the shot was more valuable than actually doing it. Rick turned his head away from the knee and I nodded. I saw Rick's finger tense and for a second I worried he might do it. The driver's scream stopped him. "Okay, okay, I'm opening it. Look!"

I watched Rob put the phone between his ear and shoulder and then twist his body so that his left hand could reach the door. He jerked the door handle and then put his left palm next to his right against the windshield.

"Let me talk to my wife."

"No." I watched as the door to the truck swung open and Rob suddenly looked to his left hard enough to give himself whiplash. I couldn't see D.B. yet, but I knew the ski-masked biker was taking the guard's gun. Rob was roughly shoved to the other side of the cab and then D.B. got in behind the wheel. Rick and I reached out and closed the van doors and Franky stomped on the gas harder than he needed to. I climbed back into the front seat and told Franky to take it easy. The van went from driving errati- cally to just dangerously. After I punched him in the arm, he slowed down and did things just like we practised. I checked the side mirror and saw D.B. behind us in the truck. My watch told me that two minutes had elapsed. We left the lot and got onto the busy road running behind the store. Forty seconds later, we were in front of the garage. Rick opened the back door and ran around the van to the garage doors. He yanked up the door on the right and D.B. slipped the truck in like Cinderella stepping into her glass slipper. Rick lowered the door and opened the second. To his credit, Franky moved in without screeching the tires.

Everyone but Donna was out of the vehicles in a heart- beat. D.B. had Rob out with a hand around his neck. Rob didn't try to fight; he just screamed his wife's name. D.B. didn't waste time fucking him up; he just shoved him back into a support beam running from the floor to the ceiling and zip-tied his hands around the pole.

"Donna, baby, I'm here. Don't worry. Everything is going to be fine, baby. Donna, you hear me? I love you, baby."

D.B. forced Rob to his knees while I tried to open the truck using the keys we pulled off Rob's belt. Everyone stopped what they were doing and looked at me while I turned the key. If it didn't work, we had to call Ruby and wait for her to show up with the keys she lifted, and that meant spending more time with the truck than anyone wanted to. The mechanism turned, the lock disengaged, and everyone got back to work. D.B. took the tape from the back of the van and put a strip over Rob's mouth before he started securing the guard's ankles to the beam. When he finished with the guard's legs, D.B. put a strip of tape over his eyes. Rick cut Donna out of the chair and gave her the same treatment her husband had gotten. We all took off our masks and D.B. joined Franky behind the truck. I started passing the money out of the back into Franky's waiting hands. The money was in tight, shrink-wrapped bundles meant for the ATM and Franky grunted each time he took one from me. Somehow he looked even more nervous than before. He was sweating like a sinner at the Inquisition and he couldn't stop looking at Rick. I threw one of the bricks at him hard enough to get his attention and when he looked at me, I showed him I had another one ready to throw. Franky understood the message and got to work. He quickly passed his load to D.B., who took each brick in one hand and tossed it into the van.

We got the van loaded in five minutes without any help from Rick. He stayed by the doors watching the street. The kid was probably worried about the cops; he didn't realize that the longer it took to load the money, the longer we had to stay near the crime scene. I closed the van doors and slapped D.B. on the back.

"I gotta admit, bro. It was a good plan," he said.

I nodded. "Let's go."

Franky got behind the wheel of the van. We had planned to let D.B. drive, but Franky must have been too jazzed up to keep his head straight.

I opened the driver side door and said, "Move over, Franky. We need to stick with the plan."

Franky shook his head and put two hands firmly on the wheel. "I'm driving," he said.

"Move the fuck over," D.B. said from the passenger side. "You know we gotta keep our shit tight."

"New plan," Rick said, turning from the doors. He was pointing the AK in our direction.

CHAPTER TWELVE

"Step away. Both of you. Keep moving until you hit the wall. When you do, turn to face it and get down on your knees."

"What the fuck, Rick?" D.B. said.

Rick shouldered the rifle and aimed it at D.B.'s chest. "Use my name again and you won't have to worry about getting on your knees — I'll put you on your back."

"Little fuck. I take it back, bro, your plan sucks balls."

I watched Rick moving the AK back and forth. The rifle would cut us both down at this range before we could get to cover. I had to do what he said until he had to lift the door. When he turned to pull the door, I would pull the Glock from the holster at my lower back and cut him down. The van would have to work to drive through the closed metal door. I would use the time to put enough rounds through the driver side door of the van to stop Franky from leaving.

"Listen to him," I said as I moved one step to my left.

"Are you serious, bro?" D.B. said from the other side of the van. "I say we rush him. He can't take us both."

"I could," Rick said.

"He's right," I said. "You don't have to be Annie Oakley to kill somebody with an AK. Think of all those kids in Afghanistan who do it everyday. Just do what he says."

"Fuck that," D.B. said.

"Recognize when you're beat," Rick said. He was looking at D.B., but the muzzle was trained on me.

"Listen," I said. "We just want to get out of here ahead of the cops. Open the door and go."

I put it out there for D.B. I wanted the kid to go for the door. D.B. got it. I saw Rick swing the gun towards D.B. and I watched the barrel inch towards the other side of the room as it followed the huge biker to the wall opposite me. I took my own steps to the left. I moved nice and slow so that I wouldn't spook the kid holding the assault rifle and cause his finger to twitch just enough to aerate my torso. The gun in the holster at my back suddenly felt like it weighed more than it did. With each step, I felt it waiting for my hand to free it. The draw would be from my knees. My hand would have to move from above my head to my waist and then back up to shoulder height. The movement would take less than a second. I watched Rick and his gun and mentally drew the Glock in my mind. I had been in front of guns so many times before that my hands didn't shake when I looked at the wrong side of a Russian machine gun. My breathing slowed and everything around me seemed to go into slow motion. I once saw a baseball player on television say that time seemed to change when he was at bat. He got into the zone, and in it, he was able to notice things that he usually never picked up on. The pitcher's finger position, the spin of the ball, the sound of the air being split by the hundred-mile projectile heading straight for him. In front of Rick and his gun, I was in the same zone. I saw the tension on Rick's trigger finger, his pinprick-dilated pupils, even the quick rise and fall of his chest. When the time came, I would see him alter his focus and I would kill him.

D.B. got to his wall before me and I heard Rick tell him to get on his knees.

"Now put your hands behind your head and lace your fingers. Now stay like that."

It was my turn next.

"On your knees," he said.

I moved slow — I didn't want Rick thinking that I gave up too easily.

"Move it. Don't make me kill you."

My knees touched the pavement and I felt cold concrete through the heavy material of the green cargo pants I wore. I put my hands up and watched Rick.

"Eyes on the fucking wall!" he screamed.

I looked back at the wall as Franky yelled out, "Let's go, man!"

I didn't need to see Rick. The noise from the door would let me know when the time was right. I waited for the sound of metal on metal, but instead I heard two loud bangs. I risked a look and saw the rifle aimed at my face.

"Eyes on the wall, motherfucker. I swear, next time you look, I pull the trigger."

Before he had even finished speaking, someone else started rolling the door up.

"Let's go," Ruby said.

She was supposed to have gone straight to the safe house unless we called. She had made a detour.

"We're all done," Rick said. The van started and I heard Franky put it in gear.

"Almost. They need to go," Ruby said.

"What?"

"Did you think we could just take the money and that

was it? I know these men. They will hunt us forever. They need to die."

"That wasn't part of the plan," Rick said.

"It was always the way it had to be and you know it," Ruby said.

There was a short silence. Rick was hesitating, but he would realize there was only one choice soon enough. For him there was no other option than to kill us. Ruby was right; if they left us breathing we would never let them get away clean.

I didn't give Rick a chance to come to his own decision — I made the choice for him. The Glock was in my hand in under a second. Rick still facing me meant that I had to make myself less of a target. Instead of staying on my knees and bringing the gun to shoulder height, I flopped onto my back, bringing my shoulder down to the gun. As I fell to the concrete, I saw that Rick had let his gun droop while he steadied himself for the final part of his betrayal. It was coming back up a second behind my pistol. I put two rounds in Rick and Ruby's direction. The slugs punched the concrete between the two doors and sent the pair running for the other side of the van.

I heard a single shot, probably from D.B.'s gun and then a burst of automatic gunfire sounded. The van started to move forward with Franky low in the seat and I put three rounds into the door and two in the side window. The tail end of a shriek leapt through the shattered window just before I heard the door on the other side of the van open. The door slammed shut as balding tires spun on the smooth garage floor. The rubber found purchase and the van shot forward out of the repair bay, leaving only black marks behind. Without the van between us, I saw D.B. again — he didn't look the same.

CHAPTER THIRTEEN

The AK had punched three dots into D.B.'s guts as though it had let a sentence trail off. The first bullet had entered just under his right lung and the third looked like it had bored into his pelvis.

"Little fucker shot me. I was wrong. The job had three problems."

"Forget that, we need to get out of here."

"No problem. I'm in the mood for a fuckin' jog."

I could hear sirens in the distance. I checked my watch and saw that thirteen minutes had passed. The sound was the first squad cars responding to the scene less than a kilometre away. Rob and Donna must have heard the sounds too. They frantically mumbled under the tape like they were doing a bad duet. I told them to shut the fuck up, and saw that they had both wet themselves.

"Stay here," I said to D.B.

"No problem, bro. Take your fuckin' time. Hey, Rob, you and your lady shut up. If I'm not complaining, you sure as hell can't."

I ran out to the lot and saw the Jeep Ruby had been driving outside the garage. The engine was still running. She had probably planned to follow the van to the safe house after her boy killed me and D.B. along with the guard and his missus. Shooting at Ruby and Rick had made them think on the fly; it was something the con artists weren't used to. They chose flight over fight and piled in the van, which was the fastest way out. With the automatic rifle, they could have killed D.B. and used the truck for cover while they took a run at me. They had better firepower and the numbers to do the job — a little patience was all that had been missing.

I got in the Jeep and reversed into the garage. I was moving so fast that D.B. brought his hands up in fear of getting run down. I got out and opened the trunk hatch. The seats went down with a little fidgeting and I hoisted D.B. inside. He screamed when I moved him. The scream wasn't through bared teeth; D.B.'s mouth was open wide and strings of spit billowed off his lips with the force of the yell. I slammed the lid and pulled out of the garage. The Jeep idled for ten seconds while I closed the door and then we were on the road.

"Press on the wounds as best you can, D.B."

"Three bullets, two hands, Wilson. Do the fucking math."

I pulled off the road into a Walmart parking lot. I took the handicap spot and said wait here to D.B.

D.B. laughed and then groaned. "Where the fuck am I going to go?" As I got out of the car I heard him say, "Get me some Smarties, bro."

The bastard was tough, but blood loss didn't care about tough. I ran inside and bought fifteen Tensor bandages meant for sprains along with some tape and gauze. I was back in the car within three minutes and D.B. was barely conscious. Shock was teaming up with the blood loss to put him out.

I drove around to the side of the building where there was only an emergency exit, pulled to the curb, and climbed over the seats to D.B.

"Hold the wound under your lung," I said while I unbuckled his belt and unzipped his pants.

"You got it," D.B. whispered.

I taped huge amounts of gauze over each of the wounds and then ripped open the boxes of Tensor bandages with my teeth.

"You got a guy you can call? A doctor for the Thieves that can keep his mouth shut?"

"Get my phone," he whispered.

I pulled the disposable phone I gave him for the job out of the inner pocket of his leather jacket and let him dial the number while I worked the bandages around his torso. He screamed loud enough to hurt my ears and told someone on the phone to hold on. I took the phone and held it against my shoulder with my ear so I could keep wrapping.

"D.B., what the hell is going on? D.B.?"

"You a friend of D.B.'s?" I asked.

"Who the fuck is this?"

"Doesn't matter. You a friend?"

"Yeah."

"He's been shot. Bad. Three times, low in the body. We need a place to take him."

"I know a guy. You need to get him to Brantford. I'll give you directions."

"No good," I said as I moved D.B.'s hand off the third shot. "The car we're in is going to be real hot real soon. You need to meet me somewhere and pick him up."

"Where?"

I pinned the bandage in place and jammed a fresh one

under D.B.'s back. He screamed louder than before as I wrapped it around his thick abdomen.

"What the hell was that?"

"Bowling alley at the end of the Lincoln Alexander Parkway. You know it?"

"Yeah. I'm sending people. You want to tell me what happened?"

"Just get to the bowling alley," I said. "I'll park around back."

I ended the call and finished wrapping. D.B. looked like half a mummy when I was done. I could already see blood getting through the bandages, but the flow had slowed considerably from the pressure of the wrappings.

"Who was that?" I asked.

"That was the Big Dawg," he whispered.

Roland "Big Dawg" Simcoe. The head of the Forty Thieves. A man in charge of an army of bikers with less sense than D.B. A man who would want some answers about what happened to his number two.

"Hey," D.B. whispered. "Where the fuck are the Smarties?"

CHAPTER FOURTEEN

Behind the bowling alley were a few Dumpsters and a chain-link fence running along the other side of the single-lane road that sat like a dry moat behind the building. Through the fence, I could see the parkway. Worse, the parkway could see me. The black Jeep wasn't hot before the job, but it was parked outside the garage. When they found the armoured truck, they might find someone who noticed the Jeep. There was also a chance Ruby could do something rash. She was panicked and on the run. She might decide to leak the Jeep to the police, hoping that they could finish what was started inside the garage with their police issue pieces. It was a stupid and risky idea; if we got caught instead of killed, we wouldn't have the money on us. Even a uniform would be smart enough to figure out that meant we had accomplices. We'd have no reason to keep Ruby, Rick, or Franky's names out of the cop's ears. Ratting was nothing but a bad idea, but so was trying to shoot us. I couldn't plan for only good ideas; they didn't seem to be in big supply today. I had to plan for anything that could happen and that meant I had to get rid of the Jeep.

I pulled in tight against the building and left the engine running.

"You still alive, D.B.?"

"Yeah." His voice was so quiet I could barely hear it over the heat blowing out of the vents.

"I know this will sound insensitive, seeing as you're shot up, but I need to know. Should I expect Roland to show up ready to kill me?"

I heard D.B. laugh. "Yeah," he whispered.

I had thought as much. Whether or not I was directly at fault, I was delivering the Big Dawg's number two all shot up. I was the messenger, and the messenger doesn't have a lot of luck in what I do. If Roland didn't try to kill me outright, he would at least want to take me for a trunk ride. He would want to know why D.B. could now be confused with Swiss cheese. If he found out about Ruby, Franky, her kid, and the money, he would cut himself in and edge me out.

"Go," D.B. said.

It was unnecessary; my mind was already made up. I got out of the Jeep and opened the trunk.

"Give me your phone," I said.

D.B. didn't move anything but his eyes. He tried to look at the floor beside him, but he only managed a glance at his shoulder. I followed the path and saw the phone beside him on the floor of the Jeep. I picked it up and touched redial. Roland picked up on the first ring.

"Yeah?"

"You coming for D.B.?"

"I got people on the way. They should be there any minute. Sit tight. We'll take care of both of you."

The both of you sounded predatory. "We're in the Jeep

parked behind the bowling alley," I said.

"Who are you? D.B. said he had something to do today, but he never gave me any specifics."

"I'm just a guy who was raised right," I said.

"What the hell does that mean?"

"It means I don't talk to strangers." I hung up the phone and patted D.B. on the shoulder. "They're a few minutes out. You were right about Roland."

"Going?"

I nodded. "I got to take care of some things."

"Ruby," he whispered.

"Her kid and Franky too. They have our money."

"Fuckers."

I nodded. "After I catch up with them, I'll find you."

"Roland," he whispered.

"I know," I said.

I closed the rear hatch and jogged around the building. Beside the bowling alley was a large furniture store — the kind that had a once-in-a-lifetime sale every other month. I crossed the parking lot and walked inside. I toured the giant store with my cell to my ear. I got Steve on the phone and told him where to pick me up.

I killed twenty minutes in the bathroom until a text buzzed my phone. The message read *Outside*. I left the washroom and walked straight out the door into Steve's Range Rover. He had the old model that still looked like it could climb a mountain. There were no heated leather seats, just worn upholstery and a roof rack.

"Rough morning?" Steve asked.

"Ruby and her kid double-crossed us."

"Hunh."

"Yep."

I told Steve where I needed to go and he pulled into traffic.

"Stupid," Steve said when we stopped at a light.

"Me or her?"

Steve took his eyes off the road long enough to give me a look. "Her. She broke the rule."

"What rule?"

"Never play another man's game."

Steve was right. Ruby was a grifter, probably one of the best cons I had ever known. She got to me using a feint I would recognize a mile out. She had me think that she was trying to use her bastard kid as leverage when she was really baiting me with the job.

A good con is better than a shrink; they can get in a person's head and get them to give up everything without having them feel like they lost anything. Ruby was better than good — she was great and she got in my head enough to know that deep down inside me there was something primal that wouldn't be able to sit still. That part of me was dying to work and she tapped into it. She knew me growing up, knew my uncle. She knew a challenge like an armoured car full of cash would give me a boner that just wouldn't go away. The sly bitch worked me and used the dumb kid, if he really even was her kid, to slowly move me into the driver's seat. I thought I saw through her. I thought I had the upper hand, but that was what she wanted me to think. The whole thing was a thirty-move checkmate that I never saw coming.

But all that guile and subterfuge didn't end with me doing the job. She went a step further than the con and tried to pull a robbery and a murder. Duping me might have been easy, but killing me is damn hard. Ruby was a trickster, not a killer. When it came time to use violence instead of grift, her plan fell apart. That thirty-move checkmate meant shit because the board was turned over and the pieces rolled out of place. Now Ruby was where she never planned to be. She, Rick, and Franky had the money, but they didn't have their endgame — they weren't away clean. There was one loose end and it was holding a gun. Ruby knew it was coming for her and she knew that all the cons in the world couldn't save her. She had given up playing chess for a new game with new rules and higher stakes. Steve was right — she dealt herself into my game.

Steve lapsed into silence. He wasn't ignoring me; quiet was just his default setting. The wordless drive gave me nothing to do but think. My mind went over the last few weeks searching for the scent of betrayal that I had missed. It became harder and harder to concentrate because of the sound. It was an angry, primal grinding that seemed to echo off the walls of my skull. The sound shook me out of my trance and I realized that it was coming from me. My jaw was tensed and my teeth were bared. The grinding of hard calcium on hard calcium was loud and the pressure was sowing the seeds of a migraine. My hand was tight on the door handle and my feet were pressing into the floor. I felt like an astronaut tensed for re-entry. The anger was everywhere. I put my hands over my face and buried my fingers in my eye sockets. I took a deep breath and forced the anger back down into whatever cage it had erupted out of. The emotion was no good to me. It wouldn't help me get anywhere near Ruby.

"Everything can get mad," my uncle had once said. "Watch this." He threw a rock at a cat eating out of a garbage can and the stone pinged off the rusted metal shell of the can. The cat leapt to the ground and raised its back. The hiss that climbed out of its throat was ferocious. The hiss said that his jungle cat ancestors weren't as far away as we might have thought. "See? The fucking cat is angry. Now what's he going to do about it? He's got two options hardwired into that feline grey matter. Fight or flight is all he knows. And where does that get him? He fights and he dies, or he runs and stays hungry. You'd be amazed how many people are wired the same way. They're on a job and someone takes a shot at them and they go to pieces. They forget everything and fall back on instinct. It's like they don't realize that they're better than a fucking alley cat. You have to force yourself to ignore feeling angry or scared. Letting those emotions run you just means you'll end up like the cat — dead or hungry. You have to learn to let yourself feel the anger without letting it change you. You learn to do that and you won't pick a fight you can't win or run away without what you came for. In our line of work, boy, going hungry isn't an option and neither is dying."

I felt my jaw slacken and the rest of me soon caught up. I was still angry, but I wasn't riding it anymore — the anger was fuelling me, not controlling me.

Steve pulled into the parking lot of a home improvement store and parked in a space near the back of the lot. I got out, thanked Steve, and crossed the parking lot to the Dodge Neon I had left there the night before. I had stashed the car in case I needed to make my own getaway. I didn't tell anyone else about the car because no one needed to hear that part of me never fully trusted anyone else. The Neon was a close looking cousin to the Honda Civic I had boosted weeks before. There were so many Neons on the road that they attracted about as much attention as birds in the sky.

I took the key out of the wheel well and drove out of the parking lot in the opposite direction of the crime scene a few kilometres away. I drove through the city until the road hit a major intersection. I saw an independently run coffee shop on the corner and pulled into the lot. Inside, there was only a man behind the counter reading the paper.

He was happy to get me two muffins and a tea without starting a conversation, and I took a seat in the corner where I could watch the lot outside with my back to the wall. I barely tasted the food as I thought things over. I had nine bullets left in the Glock and two spare magazines. The disposable cell was still in my pocket. I had shut it down and it would stay that way. Ruby knew the number and that meant I couldn't risk leaving it on. A lifetime in the business meant she knew a lot of people; some of them would know how to follow a phone. It was clear that I had underestimated Ruby and Rick, and I didn't want to do it again. I didn't want to lose the phone because it was still useful. Ruby knew the number and she might try to call it. I would check the voice mail twice a day and then shut it down again to keep it untraceable.

The second muffin was as tasteless as the first — Ruby, Rick, and Franky were all I could think about. They had all of the money and a head start. Where would they go? They could get on a plane, but the money couldn't travel with them. They couldn't bank it so soon after an armoured car job. They had to sit on it or travel with it. I had no idea what kind of roots Ruby had, but a sixty-something woman had to know a lot of people. How many would she involve in something like this? Before I finished the last of my tea, I knew what I had to do. Ruby had too many advantages — I had to take all of them away.

NEVER PLAY ANOTHER MAN'S GAME

drove to a public library and accessed the Internet on one of the computers. I found what I needed in ten minutes. I copied the numbers and addresses off the screen, cleared the browser history, and got back in the car. I drove to a nearby college and paid for a spot in the student lot. It was just about lunch time and the campus of Iroquois College was alive with activity. Near the doors, there were crowds of smokers braving the elements to get a dose of nicotine. There were also crowds of students just hanging around. The young people laughed and talked loudly and were seemingly unaware of the cold air around them. I threaded through the kids and walked into the building. I asked a guy standing in line at a vending machine for directions and then joined the herd moving in the direction he pointed. The crowd was a mixture of aggressive scents. Young men and women smelling of way too much cologne or perfume were common. Once in a while, there was also the heavy scent of a pothead doused in too much patchouli oil. I had never had a formal education, but I had spent time in schools before. When I was younger, my uncle would use my age to get into places where he otherwise would stand out. My age let me go unnoticed while I scouted jobs where a grown man hanging around would be spotted and reported immediately. To make me better at blending in, my uncle forced me to socialize with kids my own age once a week.

"I don't want you to get a best friend or anything like that. Friends are something that will get you dead. You just need to learn to blend into a crowd and sometimes that means being able to talk to people. Talking is a skill, like juggling, that can only be developed with practice. So get the fuck to the mall and practise."

I did what I was told and I learned to talk with other kids. I stood at the mall, outside convenience stores, even in school cafeterias and I learned to become part of the pack. Being in the college brought back those memories of forced interaction. It also reminded me of how much teenagers love to sit around on the ground. As I passed classrooms, I had to constantly step over feet lazily extended into the hallway. Groups of students sat on the floor in front of lockers and outside classrooms just killing time. It was something unique to the young. You never went anywhere and saw a bunch of middle-aged executives sitting on the ground and having a conversation. I checked each group for what I wanted until I found a young girl sitting with a similar looking friend who looked like she could help me out.

The girl was blonde with buckteeth, too much eye makeup, and a nose ring. She wore old Converse and tapered black jeans. The plain shirt she had on had the top three buttons open and I didn't see evidence of a bra. The friend was similar, just red-headed, better teeth, and a bra. The blonde had a sketch pad on her lap, so did the redhead.

I stopped in front of the two young women and their conversation quickly ended. The redhead looked me in the eye and turned up her lip like she was watching liposuction on the Discovery Channel.

"What?" the blonde said.

"You two want to earn a hundred bucks?"

"Ewww, gross," the redhead said.

"I'll fucking scream," the blonde said.

"Not like that," I said. I was calm and that calmed them down. "With your pads there. I need a few sketches drawn up. Can you do something like that?"

"You a cop?"

In my peacoat, cargo pants, and watch cap I looked nothing like a cop. But if the two girls thought I was, I would roll with it.

"Yeah, our sketch artist is busy so I need to find someone else. If you do a good job, there might be some steady work in it for you."

"Cool," the blonde said.

"Yeah," the redhead added.

Less than an hour later, I had sketches of Ruby, Rick, and Franky. The blonde was better than the redhead. She got two done in the time it took her friend to do just the one. All three drawings were good enough. Anyone who looked at the pictures would have no trouble matching them to the real people.

I paid the girls and left the campus. I took another look at the address I wrote down at the library and turned left out of the lot. I pointed the car towards the Escarpment and the World's End.

CHAPTER SIXTEEN

The World's End was a pub for reporters. It was heavy on print, but some of the TV reporters slummed there too. I found the bar on the web when I looked up the newspaper softball team. The bar was the team's sponsor, and they put their name on the back of the cheap jerseys.

At one in the afternoon, the bar was running on fumes. Whatever business came with the lunch crowd had gone back to work. I sat at the bar and ordered a Coke. The bartender rolled his eyes at me and slowly walked away, dragging a rag down the bar, to get my drink. Reporters drank more than cops, so a Coke was a sign that I wasn't one of their kind. When my drink came back, I noticed it was in a short glass without ice — a hint that I wasn't welcome.

The World's End was dark and everything had some kind of dark wood on it. It was a dim hole where the rest of the world could be forgotten — a place where secrets could be told. I drained the Coke and people-watched. In a booth, three men spoke loudly about LeBron James and argued about his move to Miami. Another table had a man and a woman sharing a conversation that looked like it might erupt into a make-out session at any moment. I guessed it was an office romance. Three other tables had solitary men with hard liquor in front of them. I watched the three men closely. I wrote off the one closest to me when he began nodding off. The chubby man with the beard went next. He was spending too much time on his booze. The last man was reading through a file folder, pausing only to make a note or to have a sip of the drink he kept at the far end of the table. The man was in his fifties with a white moustache and a long bald runway on top of his head. He was wearing leather shoes that had thick athletic soles. He was a guy who was on his feet a lot and was starting to feel it.

I ordered a second Coke and took it over to the man's table. I took a seat across from him; he didn't look up. His hand reached over, picked up his drink, and he took a sip without lifting his eyes from what he was reading.

"Who the fuck asked you to sit down?"

"My drink was getting warm waiting for you to offer," I said.

The man sighed and looked up from his papers. "Excuse my fucking manners. How can I help you today, sir?"

"Television or print?"

"What?"

"You television or print?"

"I'm a newsman."

"You didn't answer my question."

"The hell I didn't. I told you I was a newsman and any journalist worth his pencil knows that the papers are the only real news. Television is just window dressing. Top story followed by some fucked-up American socialite's latest escapade. No time is ever given to the real issues because real life doesn't buy ratings or sponsors. It's all big flashy shit until the flash wears off and something else spicy gets its place for a minute. That ain't news, it's Pablum for the brain-dead masses."

"So you work for the *Herald*."

"The *Hamilton Herald* is where I work. It's where I ended up after the *Globe* retired me early."

"How early?"

"A decade before I was ready to give up. Cheaper to hire young up-and-comers and run stories off the wire than to keep a real journalist on the books."

"Had nothing to do with you drinking in the afternoon?"

"Does my beverage offend? By all means fuck off then. I didn't ask you to sit down. If you have a problem with my literary process, keep it to yourself at another table."

"I'm just trying to get a sense of who I'm giving my story to."

"Story?" The reporter's eyes changed. All of a sudden he looked more alert.

I nodded. "It's too important to be handed off to some guy who drinks his lunch everyday. It needs to get out fast and where it will do the most good."

"Let me guess, your boss is a dick who mistreats his employees, maybe breaks the law a little, and you're ready to blow the whistle on the asshole. A little egg on the old man's face to show him that he can't push the little guy around."

He was close. I did want to blow the lid off something, but I didn't have a problem with my boss — I had a rat problem. Three rats hiding in a dump full of dark places. Trying to search through the garbage would get me nowhere. The rats would dig in deeper and wait me out. Better to burn the dump down and wait for the rats to come running out.

"You heard there was a robbery today?"

The reporter narrowed his eyes and gave me a hard stare. "I heard some things."

"I know who was behind it."

"Say that again," he said.

"You heard me fine."

"Why tell me? Why not tell the cops?"

"I have a natural distrust for the law."

The reporter laughed. "Who doesn't?"

"If you don't want this, that's fine. I'll find someone else and you can get back to getting lit on your lunch break."

"Let me hear it," he said.

"The job was pulled by two people. A man and woman team. The woman's name is Ruby Chu. She's been arrested a bunch of times for fraud. She'll be in the system. The guy is her son, Rick." I slid the pictures across the table to the reporter. "This is what they look like."

The reporter looked at the two pictures. "Nice drawings. You do these?"

"Sure," I said.

"How do you fit into this?"

"Not important."

"Sure it is. My boss will need more than the word of a guy I met at a bar during lunch."

"Lunch was an hour ago," I said.

"I'm a slow eater."

"Un-hunh," I said.

"I need more or this goes nowhere."

"The old lady was in the grocery store while the truck was getting lifted. Her job was to hold up the guards."

"You mean they got robbed too?"

"Hold up as in slow down. If you check the cameras, you'll see her take the keys off one of them."

"With a gun?"

"No."

"How'd she do it then?"

"Get a hold of the tape and watch it close. You might catch it."

"Will I see this guy on the tape?" he said pointing a yellow finger nail at Rick.

"No, he was wearing a mask. He was outside with a third man."

"Where's his picture?" The reporter actually sounded a little angry about a third picture missing. It was almost like he thought I had stolen something from him.

"I don't have a picture of that man. Just these two."

"How do you know all of this?"

I took a sip of my Coke and waited, letting the question evaporate.

"There's more. Another angle."

The old man looked giddy. He leaned in towards me, waiting for what I had to say.

"The job didn't start at the grocery store. The old lady and the other guy kidnapped the armoured car driver's wife. They left them in a vacant auto shop a klick away."

"Why would they do that?"

"You're the reporter. Figure it out. Far as I know none of that was released, so you're already ahead of the game."

"How do you know all of this?" he asked again.

"I'm just a concerned citizen trying to make sure justice gets served."

"Well, I thank you, mister citizen. I'm sure when this breaks you'll get that justice you wanted."

"I hope so," I said. "But don't sit on it long. The TV news will know about it shortly. You wouldn't want to get scooped."

I stood up as the old reporter sprung to life. The afternoon drinking had made him slow and shaky, so he compensated by cutting corners. He collected all of the papers on the table in a sloppy swipe and jammed them into his bag. I heard the paper crinkle as I walked away.

I watched the reporter leave the World's End from a doorway across the street. He jogged to his car with his bag under his arm and his keys in his hands. The idea of being scooped had put an expiration date on what I had told him. He had to move fast or it would spoil. Any concerns about who I was or the truth of what I had said had taken a back seat to *what if I'm not the first to tell the world*.

I got in the Neon and drove across town to west Hamilton. West Hamilton was home to the university and a boarding school for immigrant students. Students at the boarding school usually spent a few semesters learning English before moving on to the university or other nearby schools. The dense student populations that lived around the schools spawned restaurants, bars, and convenience stores that catered to them. I walked into a convenience store that advertised mostly in Chinese and bought a new prepaid cell phone. I walked back to the car and leaned against the hood while I opened the phone. Once it was set up, I called a number I had gotten while I was online at the library. I dialled and then entered the extension of the news director for SC News. The call went straight to voicemail. When I heard the beep, I said, "The *Herald* has pictures of the people who robbed the armoured car. The police haven't seen them yet. The story should run tomorrow morning on the front page of the Saturday paper. It would be a shame if you guys were left behind."

I hung up the phone and made similar calls to the news directors of the bigger Toronto stations. I also called the Toronto papers and left messages at the crime desks. By tomorrow, the story would be out. The *Herald* wouldn't be able to hold on to an exclusive for long when so many other bigger sharks were circling. The fire had started. Ruby's and Rick's names would be out along with their images. Running would be impossible. I had left Franky's picture out because he was the only link to Ruby I knew of. He wasn't a pro, so I doubted he had any connections he could rely on. I had put five rounds into the van and I heard him scream. Bleeding from a gunshot wound, he would have few options. Ruby and Rick would either dump him or kill him. I figured they wouldn't kill him, because if they wanted him dead they would have tried to do it when they went after me and D.B.

Letting him in on the plan to cross us meant there was a good chance that he was still alive. If the blood loss was severe, they would have to get him to a doctor. He couldn't go to a straight doctor — gunshot wounds had to be reported. That meant he needed someone off the books. There were a few doctors around who would do that kind of work and a few more vets who would practise on humans. Most of those doctors had legitimate practices; the illegal moonlighting was just to pay for whatever vices had taken over the doctors' lives. Franky was shot early in the morning, meaning any medical attention he got would likely take place in an office. Ruby and Rick would have dropped him somewhere. I had to find him before they picked him up again. More important, I had to find him before Ruby and Rick figured out they were famous. When that happened, Franky would be the least of their problems.

Ruby had planned her scam well. She had worked me and D.B. like a pro. But everything she did was aimed at one thing — getting her, Rick, and Franky away with the money. There would be no plan B for the end. Her plan ended with her rich and us dead. There was no way for her to fix the endgame going bad. My surviving meant she now had to plan on the fly. Putting her name and face out there along with her kid's would amp up the pressure. She would have no choice but to lay low. That would give me a chance to catch up, but it wasn't going to be easy.

The police would be behind me the whole time, looking for the same old woman. There would be bikers on the trail too. Roland had to already know what happened. The armoured car was already on the news and the Big Dawg would immediately understand where the holes in his lieutenant came from. He wouldn't know Ruby was involved until her face and name were out tomorrow. When he found out about Ruby, the hunt would begin. The cops wouldn't be able to keep up with the Thieves, who had the advantage of being full-time scumbags. They would start tearing up all of their haunts and contacts looking for a line on Ruby while the cops were still taking statements. The cops wouldn't be looking under the same rocks as the bikers — that was where I would be. I had about eighteen hours to get ahead of both cops and robbers.

called Sully's Tavern and asked Steve who was around. Steve didn't miss a beat. "The only guy you'd know is Bruce."

"Fuckin' Bruce?"

"The one and only."

Fuckin' Bruce was a bad luck charm. He never had a penny to his name because every scheme he tried always blew up in his face. Any job I heard he was a part of ended up scoring nothing but jail time. The weird part was Fuckin' Bruce never got pinched. The one bit of luck he had hovered around him like a hula hoop. Word got out that he was cursed and he spent a few years stocking shelves in a convenience store, cans only — no one let him near glass or produce — until a bunch of cons figured out how to harness the power of Fuckin' Bruce. A few underground gambling operations decided to put Fuckin' Bruce in as a cooler. No one was able to get a hot streak going when the angel of debt was in the room. His days of stocking shelves were over and Fuckin' Bruce was into some real money. He never held onto any of it, though; the money, like everything else, went south sooner than later. The irony of it all was that, despite his constant bad luck and the huge amount of misfortune he brought to other people, everyone loved Fuckin' Bruce. He was the nicest guy you could ever meet.

"Tell Fuckin' Bruce to be outside in twenty minutes. I need to talk with him."

"You sure that's a good idea?"

Steve wasn't superstitious and neither was I. We didn't believe that Fuckin' Bruce had some kind of tangible power that could stick to you if you hung around him long enough. What we did believe in was hard facts. Things went bad around Fuckin' Bruce. No one knew why, but it was the truth, so it was best to keep your distance.

"I'm not going to take a drive with him. I just want to bend his ear."

"I'll tell him," Steve said before hanging up the phone.

I drove downtown and waited a block away from the bar for Fuckin' Bruce to come outside. About five minutes into my wait, I saw him come outside. Fuckin' Bruce was maybe five feet tall with no hair on the top of his head. He grew the sides and back long into something that resembled half a mullet. He had a handlebar mustache and the hairiest arms I had ever seen. From a distance, dressed in an old parka, he looked sort of like an Eskimo child who fell asleep first at a slumber party and had part of his head shaved.

I drove up the street and double-parked beside the row of parked cars at the curb in front of Fuckin' Bruce. I rolled down the window and let him see it was me.

"Hey, man." He started around the car at the curb towards the Neon.

"Stay on the sidewalk, Bruce," I said.

"Oh, sure, I get it." Fuckin' Bruce had a look on his face like he was just picked last in gym for the hundredth time in a row. I instantly felt like I did something wrong. I never really felt bad about anything, but Fuckin' Bruce had some way of yanking on whatever short heartstrings I had left.

"I didn't mean anything by it, Bruce. You just don't want to be seen with me right now. Trust me."

"Things are hot?"

"I'm running a fever, Bruce."

"Can I help?"

"I need to know who's doing off-the-books medical care."

"You hurt? I can get you to a hospital."

If I drove with Fuckin' Bruce to the hospital, I'd never make it there alive.

"I'm looking for someone who would need a doctor, but not a lot of noise."

"Gee, I don't know a lot of guys like that, but I know someone who does. You know Ox Ford?"

I shook my head.

"Ox is a broker. He sets people up with other people."

"Sounds like a dating service," I said.

"It's something like that, man. Let's say you're pulling a job and you know there's going to be a safe. Not just any safe. One of those new models with all the bells and whistles that you wouldn't be able to crack with a jackhammer and a month. For a fee, Ox will put you in touch with a pro who can open it on the spot with his eyes closed."

"Good business," I said.

"He does alright for a guy who never has to get off his ass."

"Where can I find him?"

"He spends every day at a social club in Stoney Creek

121

playing cards. Place is on Maple. He'll be there now."

"Thanks, Bruce," I said.

"You want me to come with you? I can introduce you. Let Ox know you're on the level."

I didn't want Fuckin' Bruce anywhere near the Neon. The car was hot — with Fuckin' Bruce in the car it would be nuclear. A cop would probably rear-end me at the first light.

"Nah, it's okay. I got this. I owe you a drink next time I see you."

"Thanks, Wilson. But you don't gotta do that. We're friends, and friends look out for one another."

Fuckin' Bruce and I weren't friends. He was a good guy, sure, but he didn't mean anything more to me than the stolen car I was riding in. I would buy him a drink down the road to pay him back for pointing me in the right direction. That way, we'd be even. I had enough of doing favours for people who said they were my friend.

"I'll still buy you that drink."

"You want me to call ahead? I still got his number around somewhere."

"Nah, I'll surprise him," I said.

"Then do something for me," Fuckin' Bruce said. "Instead of the drink."

"What's that?"

"I've seen your surprises. Just don't tell Ox that it was me who gave you his name."

I grinned at Fuckin' Bruce. "It'll be our secret."

MIKE KNOWLES

CHAPTER EIGHTEEN

found the social club on Maple without any trouble. The white stucco building had not been painted in a long time and the white exterior had faded to a jaundiced yellow after years of sitting in the sun while it marinated in city dust. I parked on the street and walked inside, where immediately the natural light was absorbed and eliminated. The club was a windowless box with a bar on the far side of the room, four pool tables, six card tables, and a medium-sized mounted flat-screen. Two of the pool tables were in use and the flat-screen had a handful of admirers watching darts. There was only one card table in use, so I headed there.

The four men seated were playing euchre. The game was lively and mostly silent outside of calling trumps and passing. When the hand ended, I said, "I'm looking for Ox Ford."

Two of the elderly players introduced me to Ox when they quickly glanced at him. Ox saw the looks and sighed. "I don't know you, kid. How is it that you know me?" Ox

Ford was old, maybe in his mid-sixties, but he was young in comparison to the other men in the club. Everyone else was shrivelled, bent, and worn, but all of them still had a hard look about them. The kind of look that men who had seen combat couldn't scrub off. Ox had it too.

"Can we talk?"

"Can I finish my game?"

I nodded and watched the euchre continue. Ox looked like a guy who should be named Ox. He had a huge head; his forehead was large like Cro-Magnon man. He had a wide jaw with crooked teeth. Supporting the bovine skull was a body belonging to a smaller man. He resembled a paunchy Easter Island statue.

Ox played aggressively, calling risky trumps to keep the other two players from getting their way. In between hands, he took drags on a fat cigar. The smoke pooled above the table and smelled foul — I guessed for all his success as a broker, Ox never got away from smoking cheap stogies. The game lasted five minutes and ended when Ox played a hand alone and took four points. The old men left the cards on the table and slowly got out of their chairs to give us some privacy.

"Take a seat," Ox said gesturing to the seat across from him with his cigar.

I sat across from the old man.

"What can I do for you?" he asked as he collected all the cards into a neat pile.

"I need information."

"What makes you think that's my game, friend?"

The word *friend* had a bit of edge to it.

"What say we start with the basics. Who told you my name?" There was the unmistakable sound of a hammer being pulled back. The metal on metal click was a sound I knew well.

"You're a sly one, old man," I said. "You that good at drawing cards under the table?"

Ox spoke around the cigar in his mouth. "I don't cheat at cards, kid. Just like I don't talk to people I don't know. Now spill it. How did you find me?"

I didn't answer right away. Instead, I let Ox watch my mouth form a grin. The grin was cold and nasty; I had inherited it from my uncle. His grin had always unnerved me because I only saw it when things were going to shit. Whenever it looked like my uncle was about to step into the afterlife, that grin would show up. The grin that said, *I know something you don't*. I practised the grin as a teenager until mine matched his. It was the only memento I kept.

"Hey, someone dropped a twenty over here." My voice was loud enough to cross the room and penetrate the hearing-aid-clogged ears of the old men hanging around. All three of Ox's Euchre buddies swung their heads in our direction. Ox saw them look at us and he was forced to shrug his shoulders and grin.

The three old men walked towards us, patting their pockets while they tried to remember where they had been sitting. As they neared, Ox shifted in his seat and hid the gun from view.

"I was sitting there," said a grey-haired man, sporting an old pilled sweater over creased-front khakis.

"Must be yours then," I said.

A blue veined hand snatched the bill from my hand. If the old man knew it wasn't really his, he didn't let on.

One of the other men looked at Ox and said, "You up for another game?"

"Sure, sure, in a minute fellas. I just gotta talk to my friend here for a bit."

The three men got the hint and went back towards the

bar. Ox watched them walk away. When he looked back at me, he heard the slide of my Glock ram back and then forward. Watching the game, I had walked around a bit and saw the ankle holster Ox was wearing when his pants rode up. I had moved my own gun to my pocket while Ox was busy throwing down his winning hand. When I heard Ox cock his gun, I let the Glock out for a little air. What he thought was me shifting uncomfortably in my seat as I realized he had a gun was really something much different. My gun already had a round in the chamber; I just moved the slide so that Ox could hear it. His breath caught in his throat and all of the sureness I saw in the card game drained away.

"Who are you?" The cigar drooped in his mouth and hung like a limp dick.

"My name is Wilson. Fuckin' Bruce gave me your name."

I could see from the way that his eyes darted to the left that he knew my name.

"I knew your uncle."

I was tired of people who knew my uncle. "Then you know what's going to happen if you keep that gun on me," I said.

"I'm bringing it up," Ox said. "Don't kill me."

"Two fingers," I said.

Ox brought the gun up with his thumb and index finger like the revolver was a rotten banana peel. He put the gun on the table and pulled his hand away fast. I took off my watch cap and put it over the gun. The Glock went back into my pocket, but I kept my hand on it and the sights aimed at Ox.

"We're all friends now," I said.

Ox nodded and put his cigar in the ashtray. He seemed unsure about it. "So, uh, Fuckin' Bruce gave you my name?"

"Fuckin' Bruce said you were a broker. Said you knew everyone in town."

"Not everyone. Most," he said with pride, "but not everyone. What do you need?"

"A doctor who works off the books."

"What kind of doctor? I know surgeons, general practitioners, specialists . . ."

"All of them," I said.

"What?"

"I need all of them."

"I don't know what Fuckin' Bruce told you, but that's not how this works. You tell me what you need and I contact the other party. They have the option to agree or disagree with meeting you. Everyone is kept anonymous until they decide different. That way, both are protected. I don't give out numbers. If I did, I'd be out of business."

"You must be good at keeping things anonymous because your customer service is shit." I nodded towards the revolver under my hat.

"It's a dangerous world," Ox said.

"Getting worse by the minute."

"I'm in the business of danger," Ox said. He smiled and I got a good look at his bad teeth. "I know better than anyone."

"Then you know the Forty Thieves."

Ox made a face like he had just bit into a lemon. "Bikers. I try to avoid working with those animals."

"Business must be good if you can turn down clients."

Ox spread his arms and smiled. "I do alright and best of all, I'm my own boss."

"I'm not. I'm something of a procurer. A finder of things."

"I know who you worked for," Ox said.

I knew he would. If he knew my name, a rare thing,

he knew my resumé. He also knew that I didn't work for Paolo anymore. "I'm a contractor now, and I'm not picky like you. The guy that needs finding crossed the Thieves."

"Shit," Ox said. "Money?"

"Money and blood," I said.

The colour was draining from Ox's face; he could see where the conversation was going. "I'm getting paid to find this guy and the doctor angle is all I have. The guy I'm looking for is hurt and I need to find whoever is bandaging him up. I understand loose lips would hurt the business, but pissing off the Thieves is terminal."

"Fuck," Ox said. "Fuck, fuck, fuck. I'm finished."

"It doesn't have to be that way," I said.

"It does so. You said it yourself. I either blow it with my medical contacts or a bunch of angry bikers blow me away."

"They'd probably torture you first."

Ox ran a hand over his huge head.

"There's a third option," I said. "I don't need every number. I just need doctors who could deal with bullet wounds. Of those guys, I just need the numbers of doctors who say no."

"Say no?"

"If you ask them if they can work tonight and they say no — that means they're busy. It's the busy doctors I'm interested in."

"How does that make things better? Those guys will still know I gave you their name. Word will get out that I'm not the anonymous service I said I was and the whole thing withers and dies."

"The doctors won't see me. I'll keep my distance while I check them out. If they're clean, they'll stay that way. I just want my guy."

"You think these guys are stupid? If you show up after

I call them, they'll know who sent you."

"You think I'm some fucking thug, Ox? If I tell you they won't see me, they won't."

"Blood doesn't make you your uncle, kid."

"Count your blessings I'm not, Ox. That gun shit you pulled would have earned you a stay in the hospital. I'm not my uncle, you're right, I'm still here. I do things different than my uncle. He would have put your teeth out and a gun down your throat until your fingers got to dialling. I'm just going to force you to make a decision. You either do this my way, or I call Roland and he sends some people to talk to you. Maybe it'll be D.B. You ever meet D.B.?"

"I know who he is."

"You ever meet him?"

"No."

"You want to?"

Ox shook his head.

"Then get on the phone and tell me who's not taking patients tonight."

"What, I just call up every doctor I know and start quizzing them about their schedule? That won't seem suspicious at all."

"No, you call up everyone you've ever heard of who has done bullet work and you ask them if they're up for some on-call work tonight. Tell them there's a good chance the people you're in contact with will need a doctor and if they do, they'll pay through the nose. That way if you don't call back, they will just think everything went the way it should have. They'll be disappointed but not suspicious."

"That will take some time," Ox said.

"Then hurry the fuck up."

Ox got up and started for the bar. "Do the calls here. I want to make sure you don't get clever."

Ox sat back down and pulled a BlackBerry from his

hip. While he scrolled through the phone with his right hand, his left picked up the cigar. He put the wet end in his mouth and used a lighter to get it going again. I checked out the room and saw that a few of the old timers at the bar were eyeing us. They probably wanted a game of cards with Ox. I ignored them and listened to Ox as he started talking to someone. The first caller said, "Sure," right away. Ox said he'd be in touch and hung up. He gave me an apologetic look before he started scrolling through the phone for the next number.

The old guys at the bar must have gotten tired of waiting for Ox; they walked over to the table furthest from us and started a three-man game.

Ox kept getting yesses. He looked nervous each time, but I didn't care. I just needed one name to say no. Twenty minutes into my wait, Ox pulled a pen from his pocket along with an old receipt. He wrote a name on the slip of paper and then started looking for the next number. Another name went down on the paper right away. He struck out four more times after that before coming up with another busy doctor. The third name turned out to be the last.

Ox put the phone on the card table and stubbed out the cigar. "This one," he said pointing to the second name. "He says he's out with his girlfriend tonight. He's married and his wife only goes out once a month. He wouldn't miss fucking his mistress for anything."

"The other two?"

"Just said that they were busy."

"Write down where I can find them."

"Fine, fine. You know if this gets out, I'm dead."

"If your pen doesn't start moving, I don't like your chances."

Ox said "asshole" under his breath. I let it slide.

"The addresses you're giving me. This is their offices?"

"Yeah."

"They do house calls?"

"They might, but if we're talking a bullet wound like you said, they'd want to deal with it at their office."

"Seems risky."

Ox lifted an eyebrow. "These aren't your average give you a lollipop after your checkup kind of doctors. They moonlight with some dangerous guys mostly because they're in debt to someone worse. They could be addicted to anything — drugs, whores, gambling, whatever it is it put their services on the black market." Ox pulled the cigar from his mouth and looked at the dead end. He gave it another dose of fire from the lighter and pulled hard on the stogie until it smouldered again. He pointed the cigar across the table like a professor gesturing with a piece of chalk and went on. "Most of these guys aren't even good doctors. How could they be? How many addicts do you know that are good at what they do? They're too busy using to care about anything else. Locking a guy away in a back room isn't an issue when your waiting room is mostly empty. They would rather take care of things on their turf. These guys might be shady doctors, but you got to remember they're not workers like you. They don't want to be anywhere near a place that might suddenly be full of cops. In the office they can always make the claim that they were just doing their job and they planned to report what they saw when the patient was stable. Plus, no one is going to hire someone who can't deliver. They want to be in their office so that they have access to everything they might need. If they travel, who knows what problems they might run into. If you let a guy die, maybe his partners won't want him to go alone. You keep things in an office and the patient's life expectancy rises, as do the chances that

NEVER PLAY ANOTHER MAN'S GAME

everyone will keep their cool."

I nodded — Ox made sense. "Give me the married guy's address too."

"I told you he's fuckin' tonight, not workin'."

"Put the address down on the paper."

Ox looked around the room as if someone might suddenly come to his aid, but none of the senior citizens in the joint were giving us any attention.

When he finished writing, I said, "Get up and grab your coat."

"What?"

"You're coming with me," I said.

"That wasn't part of the deal. You said you wanted numbers and that is what I gave you. I can't get involved in anything."

Ox didn't see my foot move; he just felt it as the steel toe of my boot drove into the underside of the wicker chair he was sitting in. There was the sound of some of the woven strands under his testicles snapping from the impact and then a grunt from Ox. The sound got a lot of attention from the other old timers in the room.

"Ox?" I said. "You okay?"

I pocketed the Glock, got out of my chair, and put an arm around the back of Ox's neck. "Is it your heart, Ox?"

My hand subtly changed from caring touch to violent choke as my thumb dug into Ox's voice box. He got out a weak croak until I let up enough for him to gasp.

"I think we need to get you to a hospital, Ox."

"I'll call an ambulance," someone yelled.

"My car's out front," I said. "I'll take him."

I put more pressure on Ox's throat and whispered, "Get up," in his ear. He managed a nod. I scooped up the hat and gun and led the doubled-over man out the door to my car. A few people followed us to the sidewalk, but they kept enough of a respectful distance to never notice what was really going on. I got Ox in the car and pulled away from the curb. He was breathing heavy and I could hear him wheeze every few seconds.

"What the fuck was that?"

"I told you to get your coat. You wouldn't listen. I can't have you making any more calls until I'm done, Ox. You're a broker, which means if you get it in your head that you want to pick a fight, you could send some people to meet me when I make a house call with the docs."

"I wouldn't do that."

"Why, because we're such good friends? It doesn't matter what you would do; it's what you could do that I care about."

"I was wrong," Ox wheezed. "You're just like your uncle."

I left Ox at Sully's. I told Steve to watch him and to keep him away from the phone. Steve nodded without looking up from drying the glasses coming out of the dishwasher. I took Ox's BlackBerry and told him that he would get it back later. Ox didn't try to argue with me — dragging him out of the social club took most of the fight out of him.

I got in the car and checked the clock; it was five. If the first doc really had a hot date, his office would be closed and he'd be long gone. If he had lied to Ox because he was working late on a bit of off-the-books patching up, I would find out. I used Ox's BlackBerry to pull up Google Earth. I zoomed in on the building and accessed the street view option. I used the phone to virtually survey the building. The office was a single-floor building just off Main Street that looked to be less than 500 square feet. Google let me zoom from several different angles and I saw from the window placement that it would be easy to see if anyone was home.

CHAPTER NINETEEN

The doctor's office was dark. No one came to the door when I knocked, and no one came to investigate when I pounded. I walked around the building and scaled the fence around back to look in the windows that faced the small bit of yard. All of the windows had been frosted from the bottom to the middle. This let light in while still providing privacy to the patients who had to disrobe. Each window was dark. I walked back to the front door and looked for an alarm pad. I didn't see one from the door. The lack of an alarm didn't surprise me. The office on Percy Street was close enough to the burbs to be secured by the two locks on the door. I looked each lock over; they weren't ancient and they looked strong. The two locks would keep someone busy; the glass pane above them wouldn't. I took a look around and saw no pedestrians on the sidewalk. There were a lot of cars around so I waited for the light at the corner to turn. The red light briefly brought silence to the street. The quiet was interrupted by the sound of my elbow connecting with the pane. The impact was just a love tap and the thick peacoat muffled the sound.

I made sure the street was still clear and then snaked my hand through the broken window. The locks rolled back without any trouble and I stepped inside. Inside the office, I scanned the walls for evidence of a security system that I wouldn't have been able to see from the door. Nothing caught my eye and I didn't hear any sounds that would indicate that a sensor had been tripped. I drew the Glock and moved through the empty waiting room. There was a short hallway with three open doors. The bathroom and both examination rooms were empty. I checked every garbage can and found that they hadn't been emptied recently. None of them contained anything bloody. I walked back to the waiting room and went behind the receptionist's desk. There was a large stack of files next to a computer. I nudged the mouse and the computer woke from sleep mode. The OS prompted me to input a password. I checked the desk for anything written down, but there was nothing. I gave up on the computer and looked through each of the files. The name on the file at the top of the pile had a log from four thirty. I worked my way back in time and saw that the doc had been busy almost every hour of the day. He wasn't my guy.

CHAPTER **TWENTY**

The second doctor had an office near St. Joseph's Hospital. This doctor was doing better than the last; he had a whole house dedicated to his practice. The building was an old two-storey brick home. It looked to be at least fifty years old. Unlike the first office, this place was lit up. The lights on the first floor were out and the front door was locked. The second floor had light streaming through each window and a person moved the curtains every few minutes to check the street. There was only one car in the driveway and it was in a spot marked as reserved. The doc was working late.

I sat across the street for a few minutes watching the darkness creep down from the sky. The seasons were changing and the days were getting shorter. It was dark at six fifteen. I smiled and turned up my collar. I liked the dark. After three more window checks, I opened up Ox's BlackBerry and pulled up the second doctor's number. I dialled it on the prepaid phone I had bought earlier and waited. The phone rang three times and then a man answered.

"Yeah?"

"You got cops on the way. Tell everyone to clear out now. They're five minutes out — hurry!"

I hung up the phone and watched the building. The curtains on the second floor moved again, but this time it wasn't so casual. The man in the window pressed his face to the glass so that he could see every inch of the street. A minute later, the front door opened and a man stepped out to check the street. When he saw that it was clear, he ran back to the door, opened it, and waved frantically. Another man ran out and crossed the street. He got into a Toyota Camry parked up the street and reversed the car down the one-way street to the curb in front of the doctor's office. The guy at the door started waving again and two other guys dragged a fifth man out of the building. The two men had a shoulder under the third man's arms — he was hurt bad. The injured man's feet never touched the ground once as he was carried from the office to the Toyota. They shoved him in the passenger seat and everyone else climbed in back. The car screeched away from the curb just as the doctor emerged from the office and locked up. He ran to the car in the reserved spot and made his own loud exit. I watched him go from inside the Neon. I had no reason to rush — the cops weren't coming and the man carried out wasn't Franky.

CHAPTER TWENTY-ONE

The third doctor had an office on the second floor of a medical complex. The medical complex shared a run-down wall with a drugstore. At seven o'clock, the drugstore was still open; the medical building was locked. I parked on the street and walked around to the back of the building. Out back, there was a parking lot reserved for patients and customers. The light posts scattered around the parking lot gave off a dull glow that gave me a long shadow as I crossed the pavement. There were no cars parked near the rear entrance to the drugstore. The store was open until midnight, but it didn't look like it needed to be. I saw a counter inside the rear door but there was no one behind it; there was just a sign beside the register. Customers probably had to use the checkout near the main entrance. The only person I saw inside the store was a stock boy carrying an armful of small boxes. I could see his lack of effort from across the lot. The only cars parked out back were near the medical complex entrance. There was an Escalade, a Porsche, and a Mercedes two-door parked in the three spaces closest to the building.

There was no way inside the building without a key. Breaking in would be a bad idea. I saw a large alarm pad inside the door. I could make out the name brand on the pad and I knew that there would never be enough time for me to disarm it without a schematic in my hand. I saw that there were still lights on upstairs. No one checked the windows, but someone was up there. The three cars could have all belonged to doctors, but the black Escalade had mob written all over it. I pegged the white Porsche 911 as the doctor's car, and the black two-door Mercedes as upper management of whoever was riding in the Escalade. Two doors says something. It says, *I don't ride with a crew, ever, so what do I need more than two seats for?*

I found a chunk of concrete that came from a pothole in the asphalt and picked it up. I hefted the rock and judged it to weigh about three pounds. I walked to the passenger side of the Mercedes so that the car blocked the view from the back door of the drugstore. I took a step back, wound up, and launched the rock through the passenger side window. The cold evening air was quiet — only the sounds of cars driving by the other side of the building could be heard. The sound of three pounds of concrete shattering a window was like the strike of church bell on a lazy Sunday afternoon. It echoed in the lot as the remaining pieces of glass fell inside the car and onto the pavement.

I unlocked the door and got into the car. When I leaned across the seats to get at the panel below the ignition, I snuck a look up through the windshield to the second floor. I could see someone upstairs gesticulating wildly at the Mercedes. I had chosen the car on purpose. Management drove a two-seater. Management also sent underlings to stop people from breaking into their car. I slid back from the steering wheel and got out of the car. I left the door open and stepped into the shadows formed by the corner of the building meeting the fence separating the parking lot from its identical twin on the other side. The corner of the lot was out of the reach of the light posts; it was a small patch of midnight at seven p.m.

My heart wasn't beating fast to begin with, but in the darkness it slowed even more. My knees loosened with my shoulders and I relaxed into stillness. I was there in the corner, but no one would see me. A hungry cat walked along the top of the fence on its way to my spot. I watched as it quickly padded towards my shade. I didn't try to shoo the cat or hiss angrily to alert it. I let the cat come. The cat got within five feet of me when a loud bang froze it in its tracks. The bang was easy to identify; it was the sound of the glass door of the medical complex bouncing off the brick exterior of the building. The cat gave the sound a moment's consideration before it dashed the few remaining feet in search of a hiding place. The cat got to the end of the fence and was about to jump down when it suddenly froze again. I saw the cat twitch as though it had stepped on a live wire — it had gotten my scent. I reached out and plucked the feline off its perch. The cat tried to wriggle away as it hissed an angry warning, but my hands closed around its throat, silencing it.

Two men came into view; the cat didn't notice them — it was too busy struggling. The men were textbook mob — big, leather jackets, crooked noses. Their skin was light, lighter than something that could have been produced off the coast of the Mediterranean. What I saw looked like it had roots closer to the Crimean Sea — they were Russian muscle. They both went straight to the Mercedes and bent to look inside. I had been rough with the car and the two Russians gave it some consideration. The first one to give up, a large man with a shaved head and a small patch of hair sprouting from his chin, stood and scanned the lot. I watched him notice the light from the drugstore and the stock boy inside. I could imagine the wheels turning in his thug brain. After a few seconds, he said something in what sounded like Russian to the other man. There was a short reply from his partner, who was still leaning into the car, and then the bald guy started for the drugstore.

The second man got out of the car and pulled out a cell. He hit a few keys and then held the phone to his ear. Whoever was on speed dial picked up fast. There was a conversation in rapid Russian and the thug seemed to only be able to keep up by firing off answers in short one-word bursts. I considered the thug and what was upstairs. The doctor could have had more than one patient. Ruby could have gotten Franky to the doctor before the Russians showed up. Having two off-the-books patients at once seemed like a really bad idea, but no one would tell the Russian mob that there was no room for one of their guys. My gut told me that Franky wasn't upstairs, but I had run out of doctors — I had to be sure.

I interrupted the Russian by lifting my foot and ramming it back into the building. The rubber sole of my boot did little to prevent the impact from running up my leg, but the thick cushion of the boot did make the sound little more than a dull thud. It didn't carry like the sound of breaking glass, but it did get the attention of the Russian on the phone.

He whispered something to whoever was on the other end and then put the phone away. The Russian wasn't stupid; he reached inside his coat and freed a pistol from the small of his back. He took a low, two-handed grip and approached the shadows where I stood. I watched him as he moved towards me. The Russian was a little over six feet tall and more than two hundred pounds. He had a

142

well-trimmed beard and hair that hung down over his eyes like a pre-teen pop star. He edged closer to the corner of the lot, each step bringing the gun up more. When the gun was almost chest high, I threw the cat.

The small animal was scared and oxygen starved; it made a guttural sound as it passed through the air between the goon and me. I flattened against the side of the building in case the Russian pulled the trigger in fright, but nothing happened. The man jumped back, avoiding the feline projectile, and the cat missed him by a few inches. The man cursed at the cat — I knew enough Russian to recognize the words — and lowered his gun. I heard him breathe a sigh of what must have been relief as the adrenalin faded, and watched him turn around.

I stepped out of the darkness into the dim light of the parking lot and closed the distance between me and the relieved Russian. He didn't hear me get in close; he just felt it when my hand closed around the Sig P220 he was holding. My left hand braced his wrist, locking it in place, while my right hand wrenched the barrel of the gun down. The Russian's finger lost its connection with the trigger as the Sig pitched forward and out of his hand. The gun was at the back of the Russian's head before he even had the chance to turn around.

The man knew better than to scream. The second he felt the gun against his scalp, he stopped trying to recover it. He just lifted his hands away from his hips and opened his fingers. I took hold of the collar of his jacket and walked him back into the darkness. As soon as the black tide rolled over his face and erased him, I spoke into his ear.

"Who's upstairs?"

"Fuck you." There was little accent in the curse.

"This just isn't your day. You must have a black cloud above your head," I said.

"No, I just have a gun pointed at my head."

"You're right. It's probably not bad luck that got you in this situation. Your partner had enough brains to figure out the drugstore was still open and that someone might have seen something. You lacked the smarts, or maybe the initiative, to do something other than stay with the car."

"The boss said to protect the car."

"No doubt, but why you? Why not the other guy? You keep your mouth shut and your mind closed and you'll be guarding the car until it finally blows up in your face."

"There's a bomb in the car?"

I sighed. "What I mean, genius, is that the ones who think for themselves get ahead and make money. The ones who worry about the car get treated like really cheap bomb-defusal robots. You need to be smarter starting now. Tell me who is upstairs with the doc before I decide that I should be dealing with your partner instead of you."

The Russian gave it some thought. "Why do you want to know who is upstairs?"

"Don't worry about that. Worry about the gun to your head. You have ten seconds to tell me what I want to know, or I'll show you how little your brain is when I splash it out in front of you."

The Russian didn't have to think as long. "Oleg is upstairs with Pavel."

"Not them, the other one up there."

"Other? There is no one but Oleg, Pavel, and the doctor."

Neither name made any sense to me. The Russians were under new management since I put Sergei's lights out. The men who had stepped into power had made more changes by making quick promotions so that they were backed by loyal men. I didn't know any of the new players, but I did know that the men pushed out of their jobs weren't too happy about it. Russian bodies had been showing up in the streets over the past few weeks and doctors like the man upstairs were probably working more than usual.

"The doc been there long?"

"Since this afternoon. Oleg had him close early so that he could see Pavel."

The news that I had hit another dead end came just as the Russian's partner walked into view. He circled the car calling out the name Josef.

"That you?" I whispered.

Josef nodded slowly. I could feel him push harder against the gun with each nod — he was building up momentum for a move against me. I put the sole of my boot against the back of Josef's knee and put him on the ground. My hand left the collar of his coat and found his mouth. I put the Sig to Josef's temple and waited for the smarter Russian to make a decision. He could stay outside, or go inside. From the way he shook his head after he said Josef's name again, it was clear that he was pissed that his partner had left his post. I watched him look around the lot and call out again; I also saw him close his jacket tight around his neck. The cold was all around. Part of me felt it too, but it was a part my brain refused to acknowledge in the dark corner of the lot.

After a minute, the Russian got fed up with standing around. I figured he was tired of waiting outside while the idiot he worked with was probably inside telling the boss some lie about how he had run off whoever broke into the car. The Russian took one final look around the lot and then walked towards the doors. I heard the door hit the wall again as the mobster went inside.

"Walk," I said.

Josef hesitated a second and then got to his feet with his hands in the air. He was off balance without the use of his hands and I gave him a jab in the back of the head before he was able to get his footing. The blow was hard enough to make him stumble forward. He stayed where he was, waiting for me to tell him what to do next. I didn't say another word. When he finally got the guts to turn around, he would see that I was gone. The six-foot-tall wooden fence was drilled into the bricks of the building. The posts didn't creak once when my body went up and over.

I ran out to the street and slid behind the wheel of the Neon. A few seconds later, I was rolling — where, I had no idea.

CHAPTER TWENTY-TWO

The only place for me to go was back to Sully's Tavern. I parked across the street and went inside, bringing enough cold air with me to get everyone's head to turn away from the television.

Steve was behind the bar and Ox sat on a stool across from him. Steve was in his usual khakis and white V-neck. His shaggy hair hung down over his eyes and for a second I wondered how he got anything done. Ox didn't look the same. I sat on the stool beside him and said, "Where'd you get the shiner?"

Ox stared at the drink in front of him.

I gave Steve a look.

"Tried to leave," he said.

I laughed. Ox must have thought that the wiry little man behind the counter wouldn't have been able to keep him inside. A lot of people had made the same mistake; just getting a black eye made Ox one of a lucky few.

"You know Ox here knows everybody?" Steve asked.

"He tell you that?"

"Told me that he knew people who would make me sorry I ever lived."

"And all you gave him was the shiner?"

"Figured you needed him."

If Ox objected to us talking about him, he didn't say. The old man was still giving his drink his full attention.

"You threaten him, Ox?"

I didn't get a response.

"Can I get a Coke?"

Steve nodded and walked away to get my drink. I leaned in close to Ox's ear and he flinched a little. "You know everyone, so you should understand what I am about to say. That man there is what happened to Tommy Talarese. I would give some thought to what you said and how you want to leave things with the bartender."

Tommy Talarese was once a made man. He was violent without a hint of self-control or compassion. Tommy took an interest in Steve's bar and when Steve wouldn't play ball, Tommy kidnapped his wife. I followed Steve on the killing spree that followed. Tommy's entire family died that night. Steve was something Tommy never understood. The little bartender had the restraint of a hand grenade. Without his wife to keep him in check, the pin was lost for a day.

Ox remembered Tommy. He knew all of the stories. Hearing that the man who killed that monster was the one he had just threatened made his lip quiver.

When Steve came back with my Coke, Ox blurted out, "I'm sorry. I lost it for a minute and I said some things I shouldn't have."

Steve gave him a long look. The bartender's shaggy hair was in front of his eyes and it was impossible to tell exactly what he was looking at.

"It's cool, Ox" was all he said before walking away to

leave us to talk business.

"Any luck out there?" Ox asked.

I shook my head.

"Can't say that I'm sorry about that."

"You really tell Steve that you know everybody?"

Ox nodded and drank a little.

"Do you?"

He took another sip from his drink and set it down. "I know a lot of people."

"You know Ruby Chu?"

The question tickled something inside Ox's brain. He turned his Cro-Magnon head away from his glass and gave me his full attention. "Sure."

"Well?"

"Well what?"

"Do you know her well?"

"Well enough. How well can you really know a con woman?" Ox spoke the truth.

"Let's say Ruby was in trouble and needed a doctor."

"What kind of trouble?"

"The bloody kind, Ox. She needs someone who can patch someone up and who will keep their mouth shut. Who might she go to for help?"

Ox stared at me. "What, no threat?"

"The threat is implied, Ox. If you need proof, I'll hurt you," I gestured at Ox's black eye, "but I won't be as good to you as the bartender. Now think. This would have to be someone she knows. Someone she trusts who can do the work."

"Give me my phone back."

I handed over the BlackBerry.

Ox saw me still looking at him. "Now give me some time to think."

I took a seat and spoke with Steve while Ox scrolled

through his phone. After a couple of minutes, he came up with something. He tilted the phone and showed me a name. I had never heard of Ken Parish.

"Did you call him earlier?"

"No."

"Why not, Ox?"

"This guy isn't a doctor. He was an army medic. You asked me for doctors; besides, he doesn't do any medical stuff for cash. He used to hire on to jobs as a driver. It's been a while since I've talked with him, but he's still out there, as far as I know, and he and Ruby were tight back in the day. Last I heard, he retired and bought an old place in the country. I guess Ruby might try him if she was in a bind."

I had Ox draw me directions to the Ken Parish's farm on a napkin.

When he finished, he sighed. "We done?"

"Almost," I said. "Steve, watch him a bit longer."

"You motherfucking cocksucking bas—" Ox shut up when Steve leaned an elbow on the bar and tilted his head so that Ox could see his eyes.

"No problem," he said.

MIKE KNOWLES

pulled into an Esso three blocks from the bar to gas up the Neon. The pumps had a line three-deep at eight o'clock in the evening — everyone was gassing up for Friday night. I played with the radio station until I caught the end of Miles Davis playing "Basin Street Blues." The song ended too soon and it was followed by some woman doing her best impression of Ella Fitzgerald. The vocals on the cover were in key, but she didn't have the same emotion lurking behind the words. In jazz, like everything else, attitude was what counted.

Once the tank was full, I went inside to pay. I handed over the cash and then stepped over to the Tim Hortons counter that had sprouted up between the magazine rack and the refrigerated glass shelves. It wasn't until I walked back out into the cold air with two bagels and a milk that I saw the two cops giving the Neon a once-over. Without breaking pace, I angled to the right and stepped onto the sidewalk. The cops didn't pay any attention to me; they were getting back into their car. They backed the cruiser across the lot and parked next to the air pumps, giving the Neon their full attention. I had boosted the plates and changed them with the originals. The police had obviously run the numbers and come up with an alert. They would wait until someone got in and then run them down before the next light. I crossed the street and lost sight of the police; they would be waiting a while.

It took five minutes for me to get back to Sully's Tavern and another thirty seconds for me to get Steve's keys.

The bartender laughed at me when I told him what happened. "You let Fuckin' Bruce in the car."

I shook my head. "He rested his elbow on the door when he was talking to me," I said.

"Lucky you didn't let him in," Steve said.

Ox broke into the conversation. "Not for me."

Steve flashed Ox a look and the old man went back to staring at his drink. Steve threw his keys to me and I went behind the bar to the rear exit. The windshield of the Range Rover in the rear lot was covered in a layer of hardened frost that took me a few minutes to scrape off. The engine shrugged off the cold without trouble, and it didn't take long for the heaters to start thawing the air inside the old suv.

I drove up the Mountain past Stoney Creek on my way to the rural town of Binbrook. Binbrook had once been nothing more than farmland, but over the past few years housing developments had started to take root and grow. The new houses with their identical facades spread like weeds, erasing acres of fertile land each year. Ken Parish's house was off the main road in what could only be described as old-school Binbrook. Instead of being separated by small patches of manicured lawn, the houses had acres of grass and trees between them. I found the house when I passed by a mailbox mounted on the street with his name painted right on the side. I pulled to the side of the road a little up the street where a group of trees would conceal the Range Rover from anyone in the house. The property line separating Ken's land from his neighbours was marked with a dense row of trees and brush. The neighbour had given up on farming a long time ago and had just committed to letting everything grow over. I stepped into the dense growth and wove my way through it until the lights from the farmhouse were visible. Someone was definitely home — there was smoke coming from the chimney and an old red Ford pickup parked in the driveway. The house was set on a big rectangular plot of land that stretched back a long way to more overgrown trees and brush. The field behind the house was empty and I could see a lone scarecrow up on a cross, guarding nothing. The front lawn was almost equally barren. Ken had let only grass grow outside his door. There were no trees or hedges to block his view. He would be able to see all the way to the road, without trouble, from any room in the front of his house.

I didn't want to risk just walking across the lawn to the front door. Ox had said the man inside the house had been an army medic before becoming a wheelman. A guy like that would be good with a gun. He would be on edge if he had Franky in there, and I didn't feel like getting picked off before I got inside. I kept moving through the trees until I was parallel to the house, and out of view from the windows. To be safe, I moved behind a tree and powered up the BlackBerry — the trunk would block the light given off by the screen. I pulled up Ken's number and touched dial. I took off as soon as I heard the first ring. Wherever Ken was standing in the house, his attention wouldn't be on the windows — it would be on the phone. By the second ring, I had covered the fifty metres between the trees and the house. No one had picked up the phone yet. As I passed the kitchen windows, I took a peek inside and saw no sign of anyone. I left the window and had made it to the back door when a man picked up.

"Hello?"

The owner of the voice sounded old and a bit drunk.

"I'm sorry," I said. "I think I have the wrong number. Is this the Davis residence?"

"No, I'm sorry. It's not."

"Oh, my mistake," I said as I looked in the back window. "Could I trouble you to tell me what number this is? I don't want to disturb you again if I have the wrong number."

Ken rattled off his digits with only a little slurring while I tried the knob — it turned and the door opened. God bless the country life.

"I'm sorry," I said. "I hit a six instead of a five. Sorry to have bothered you. Goodnight."

I heard Ken say, "Goodnight," but not in the phone. His voice came from somewhere on the first floor.

I was standing in a mud room connected to the kitchen. The voice had come from beyond the kitchen — probably the living room.

I powered down the phone and exchanged it for the Glock. The mud room was a small rectangular space with a mat beside the door for shoes. I saw dirty workboots, old running shoes, and a newer looking pair of Crocs. All of the footwear was the same size and they suggested that Ken was the only one in the house. As I stood in the mud room, I began to notice the background noises of the house. I heard the faint sound of a television — something with a laugh track. I also heard a clock beating out a relentless annoying ticking in the kitchen. Ken coughed a few times until he got something up and then he sighed. I waited in the room beyond the kitchen, watching the doorway that

MIKE KNOWLES

led into the kitchen from the living room in the reflection of the microwave door. Seconds lapsed into minutes, and minutes turned into an hour. Each breath I took stretched longer and longer until I was breathing in only four times a minute. The house continued to make its sounds — I was silent as the grave. When Ken had gone twenty minutes without making a noise, I stepped into the kitchen. I moved over the white-and-black checkerboard tile, careful to keep my feet close to the wall. Structurally, the floor was strongest near the walls and therefore least likely to creak and warn Ken that I was in his house.

I made it through the kitchen without making a noise, but when I stepped on the hardwood floor of the living room the boards responded with a whine. I froze where I was and watched the sleeping body of the man on the couch. Ken was about six feet tall, judging from the way his legs dangled over the arms of the loveseat. He had white hair pulled into a braided ponytail and a thick goatee. The moustache was stained yellow with nicotine. He wore cargo pants and an old T-shirt that was too faded to read. In front of the man, on the coffee table, was a bottle of Jack Daniel's. There wasn't much of the coppery liquid left. Ken snored quietly and if I had been his wife, I might have covered him with a blanket. Not being his wife, I walked past him, deeper into the room, barely lifting my feet to avoid making noise. The floor handled my presence without further complaint and Ken's snoring didn't change.

The stairs were just to the right of the front door and on the mat were a pair of high-top running shoes. They weren't the same size as the shoes at the back door and they didn't look like the kind of shoes a man like Ken would wear — I had seen the shoes before. I started up the stairs. It didn't matter how hard I tried to be silent, the wood under me crackled like wood in a campfire. I took the steps two at a time and Ken did his part by keeping his eyes shut and his ass on the couch.

I moved from empty room to empty room until I found the one guest in the house. Franky lay in a small bedroom on a pullout couch. His shirt and pants were off and I saw bandages all over his core. Judging from the blood stains on the gauze, it looked like the bullets had messed up his left lung and abdomen.

I stood over Franky watching him take shallow breaths. He was sleeping peacefully until I slapped him across the face with the side of the Glock. The gun immediately opened a gash on the side of Franky's face. His eyes opened first followed by his mouth. Only his eyes got to register the pain. My hand covered his mouth hard enough to make the springs underneath him compress.

"How you doing, Franky?"

Suddenly, my hand fell away. There was a searing pain on the back of my head and I heard someone say, "He's better than you're going to be, boy," before I heard nothing else.

MIKE KNOWLES

CHAPTER TWENTY-FOUR

I came to sitting in an uncomfortable position. The hard wooden chair under me dug hard into my spine; I tried to readjust, but my hands and feet couldn't move. My fingers explored the bindings and I realized that they had tied me tight. The rope was thick and the knots were complicated. My gun was gone and I could feel a lump pulling at the tight skin of my scalp. Franky was in front of me, still on his futon. He was awake now and propped up on some pillows so that he could see me.

"Hey, Franky," I said.

Franky's half-lidded eyes blazed for a second and I noticed a new bandage over the wound I had opened on his face. He wasn't happy to see me.

"Where are Ruby and Rick, Franky?"

"Fuck you," he said. The words seemed to seep through his clenched teeth.

"They coming back for you?"

"I don't think you need to worry about them."

I turned my head to the doorway and saw Ken standing

there.

"Doctor Parish, I presume."

"Funny, but I'm no doctor, just an old grunt. I could never prescribe anything that didn't come in a rucksack, but I can patch a man up — the army taught me that much. Know what else the army taught me? How to sleep light."

Ken came into the room and stood behind me. His two hands gripped my shoulders and began to roughly massage them. When I next heard his voice, it was right in my ear. "Are you the one who shot up Franky?"

"Yeah." Franky's voice was so low it was hard to hear.

"Franky tried to make off with my money," I said. "He got himself shot."

"Your money. It was an armoured car's money, if I heard the story right."

"Possession is nine-tenths of the law," I said.

"You stole it from them and he stole it from you. How mad could you be at someone who did exactly the same thing you did?"

"Plenty," I said.

"So you believe in honour among thieves?"

"I believe in getting paid."

"Not revenge?"

"Revenge doesn't pay the bills."

"I believe in revenge, boy. I'm serious about it, like a religion, and I know some other people who will share my interest. Believe me, they can't wait to see you again."

I felt a sharp pain in the side of my neck like a bee sting. I turtled my neck into my shoulders instinctively and the insect went away. The pain faded away fast as the futon went out of focus. My eyes started to have trouble staying open. Finally, everything went black.

MIKE KNOWLES

The taste in my mouth was what woke me. My tongue was dry and every time I swallowed, I re-sampled the stale, rotten flavour. I opened my eyes and the futon was in focus again. Franky was still in bed, but no longer propped up; he was lying flat with his head on a single pillow. Ruby Chu sat in a chair next to the bed holding his hand.

"You've been a bad girl, Ruby," I said.

She looked up from the bed and found my eyes. "Look what you did to him."

I looked around the room. The walls were white and there was a television on top of a chipped and scuffed stand in the corner.

"He needed his hand held all the way through the job. What made you think he'd be able to help you pull a double cross?"

Ruby ignored my question. "He won't wake up. Yesterday, he made jokes with me, funny jokes, but now he won't wake up."

"Bullets tend to make people do funny things, Ruby."

She dropped Franky's hand and lunged towards me. "Don't you make jokes about this. My son is dying because of you."

"Son? You said Rick was your son."

"They're both my sons."

I hadn't seen it. Ruby must've known I wouldn't, otherwise she would have never let Franky be a part of the job. Other than skin tone, Franky didn't have any of Ruby's features; he took after Ken and his Anglo ancestors. I laughed loud and long. The sound was unnatural in the room and it made Ruby uncomfortable enough to take a step back. "Very fucking sly, Ruby. Is my uncle really the father of your oldest?"

She picked up Franky's hand again. "No, Ken is their father."

"So it was all bullshit from the start. Why?"

"I needed the money," Ruby said.

"You did, or Rick did?"

"Rick did," she said. "He owed the triad. That much was true."

"How much did he owe?"

"More than his share."

"So you decided to cut me and D.B. out."

"I had no choice. I told you, a mother will do anything to protect her child."

Ruby stood up and walked towards me. "How did you find Franky?"

"It's what I do, Ruby. I find people."

"And you kill them. That's what you came to do, isn't it? Kill my son?" Ruby pulled my Glock from the front pocket of her hooded sweatshirt and put it against my temple.

"I came for my money," I said.

"Too late. The money is all gone." The front sight of the gun dug hard into my skin and I felt a trickle of blood roll down my cheek.

"Then you're in some trouble," I said.

Ruby laughed. It was a witch's laugh, full of malice and evil. "I think you have it backwards." She pressed the gun harder against my head and pursed her lips.

"You check the news today?"

The question fazed her. "What?"

"The news. Did you watch it?"

"I've had more important things going on."

"Before you pull the trigger, you might want to turn on the television."

"I know what we did will be on the TV. I always knew that."

"It's better than that, Ruby. Turn on the TV and see if you still want to kill me."

I knew it wouldn't take much to get Ruby to postpone killing me. I had felt the gun shaking against my head. She didn't have the guts for up-close wet work.

She placed the gun on the edge of the futon and walked over to the television in the corner. She found the local news channel and waited, with her back to me, for the commercials to end. She had said Franky had been talking yesterday, meaning it was now today. I said a silent prayer to whatever gods watched over people like me that it was late enough for the morning news to be on. The news came back on and I watched the highlights from last night's Leafs game through the gap between Ruby's elbow and her body.

"What time is it?"

Ruby didn't turn to look at me. "TV says five forty-five."

"Wait for the headlines at six."

"We'll see," she said. Her voice was monotone, almost robotic.

We watched the sports and celebrity highlights. The final commercials before the headlines came on when Ken came back.

"You didn't do it."

"Not yet."

"Why not? What the hell are you doing?"

"Just wait," Ruby said. "Something isn't right."

A third voice sounded in the room. This voice was reverberating with rage. "What's not right is that this motherfucker is still breathing."

I heard Rick coming across the floor; I knew better than to look in his direction. The punch would be coming and meeting it face first would be just stupid. I shrugged my shoulders and the punch glanced off the top of my skull. The second punch was a hook to the back of my head. The force of the blow sent the chair tilting forward on two legs. I hung in the air, between falling forward and back, until the momentum ran out and the chair slapped back down again. Rick stepped in front of me cradling his right hand. The punching was over and the kicking was just getting started.

"Motherfucker, motherfucker, motherfucker." Rick kept swearing and kicking. The first was the worst; every subsequent kick had less fire behind it. The kicks kept pushing the chair backwards, tilted on the rear legs, a few inches at a time. I took the fourth kick in the chest and gave it a little extra juice with my feet. The chair went over and broke on impact; Rick's feet followed me to the floor like an angry swarm of bees. The kicks to my head had me seeing white fireworks and losing sight of the futon all over again. The beating only ended when Ruby yelled, "Oh my God! David, look at the television!"

I saw Rick, who apparently also answered to David, wind up again, but Ruby grabbed a hold of him and twisted his face towards the small television in the corner.

"Holy shit," he said.

I could hear the news anchor in the sudden silence:

> *Hamilton Police have confirmed that they have two suspects in yesterday's brazen robbery of an armoured car on the Hamilton Mountain. Information on the identity of the robbers given to the Hamilton Herald has been confirmed by Detective John Campbell. The suspects are Ruby Chu and her son Rick Chu. Police will not say the role each played in the robbery, but anyone with information about the pair is asked to call Crimestoppers or the Hamilton Police.*

"Holy shit, they have our pictures," David said.

Ken shushed him.

> *Police have released the following footage from inside the grocery store yesterday morning. In the circle you can clearly make out one of the suspects. Police say Ruby Chu is known to police and sources say that she has an extensive criminal record.*

The video of Ruby in the store played on the screen. The news was nice enough to put a highlighted circle around Ruby while she lifted the guard's keys.

When the next story started, everyone turned around to look at me. Their faces all had the same look of bewilderment. That was good. It meant none of their faces had to change when they saw me on my knees holding the Glock.

CHAPTER TWENTY-SIX

Ken might have been a good medic and a light sleeper, but he was shit at tying people up. Instead of binding my wrists together, he had tied my arms to the chair by wrapping the rope around my body; my feet were wrapped the same way. When the chair went over, the frame broke and the rope loosened enough for me to move my hands. I was able to shimmy my way back across the floor to the futon while Ruby, Ken, and their boy watched themselves on the news.

The beating had been loud enough to rouse Franky from his sleep and he had managed to prop himself up on his elbow. His eyes were wide as he watched me coming for the gun Ruby had left on the futon. He tried to mouth words of warning to his family, but he didn't have it in him.

Every inch was a fight. I was swallowing mouthfuls of blood and spit and I had to constantly wipe my eyes on my shirt so that I could see. I got to my knees as the video of Ruby in the grocery store started playing. I made eye contact with Franky and gave him a painful wink before twisting my body and picking up the gun Ruby had pointed at my head a few minutes before.

The rope was still wrapped around my body and there were still parts of the chair hanging off my back. There was just enough slack for my hand to get a hold of the gun. I held the Glock at my side the same way Bogey used to in the movies. It wasn't the way I wanted to hold the gun, but if it worked for Philip Marlowe, who was I to complain?

Eight eyes were all on me and the barrel of the gun aimed at Rick's groin; I said, "Let's talk." The words fell out of my mouth and I heard myself slur the *S* and the *T* so that it sounded like "Letshstalk." If anyone had any trouble understanding me, they didn't say anything.

"Turn off the television," I said.

"How did they get our pictures and my name?" Ruby demanded.

I shot the screen. Ruby and Ken jumped a second too late. The bullet had already travelled between them and bored its way through the TV. David started backing away from the gun, but I waved him back to his family.

"Sit on the floor," I said.

This time no one said anything. Everyone did as they were told.

"I gave the papers your name and picture. They know all about you."

"You son of a bitch," Ruby hissed.

"You try and kill someone, make sure they die. The living have a hell of a way of fucking things up," I said.

Ruby's lips quivered and she started to cry. Ken reached for her and I said, "Stop."

"What the hell are we going to do?" David asked. "I'm not going to jail."

"Jail is the least of your problems." That got me a look from everyone.

"You going to shoot us?" Ruby said. Her face was a wicked mask of anger and hatred.

"I don't mean me. Junior here shot D.B. up, but he didn't finish the big guy off. You've got a few hours until Roland reads the paper. By then, you might be better off just turning yourself in."

"Who the hell is Roland?" Ken asked.

David shrugged.

"Tell them, Ruby."

Ruby's mouth stayed shut. Her eyes said it all; they were glassed over with tears. Eventually, the water crested and spilled down her cheeks.

I sighed and swallowed a mouthful of blood. "Roland is in charge of the Forty Thieves. D.B. is his lieutenant. Your son shot D.B., Ken. Roland didn't know what kind of job his second in command was moonlighting on, but he sure as hell knows he was shot up. He would have figured out how it happened when he heard about the armoured car, and when he reads the papers, he'll know who did it. He'll be looking for you two. Bikers love settling scores. He'll want the money too — all of it. He'll take it personal that you used one of his guys and never cut him in. When he hears that it was you two that did it, he'll come looking for his cut and to make a few cuts of his own."

Ken whirled on David. "Is this true? You shot a *biker*?"

"Ma said we had to. There was no other way to get the money."

Ken looked at Ruby. "How could you let this happen?"

"Let? We didn't have a choice. He needed the money and it was the only way."

Ken shoved David. "The money! The money! Look

what happened because of your stupid gambling. As if gambling hasn't cost us enough."

"What is he talking about?" I asked.

"None of your business," Ruby snapped.

"No, why shouldn't the man with the gun in my house, the man who shot my Franky, why shouldn't he know about that?" Ken looked at me; his face was flush. "Why do you think she's still working? Why do you think she's gone so low that she has to fake cancer? She's broke. She gambled everything away. And this one," he said pointing to David with a finger shaking with anger. "He picked up right where she left off. Except he wasn't happy with bingo and slots. No, he played for big money and lost more than his mother could have if she had twenty more years and four more hands for stamping those fucking cards."

"You drank everything you had," Ruby shouted. "Don't act like you're better."

"But I still have my house. I didn't swallow that. What do you have?"

"You don't own your house, Ruby?"

Ken laughed. "She doesn't have a house. When she's not convincing people to donate money for her expensive treatments the horrible government won't sponsor, she's out conning her way into other people's houses. She finds terminal cases in the hospital with no family and steals their keys so she can sell off everything they own while she squats."

I pointed the gun at Ruby and she started to creep backwards. "Goddamn," I said. "It was so perfect, I didn't see it. You were penniless, cancer stricken; the only thing you had left was a house. And what did I need? A fucking house."

Ruby wouldn't meet my eye.

"Look at me."

MIKE KNOWLES

She shook her head. I twisted my torso and felt my body complain. After a few twists, the rope and the pieces of chair tied to my back fell to the floor. I lifted the gun until it was pointed at the frail body on the bed.

"How about now?"

Ruby flashed me a look probably expecting to see the gun in her face. When she saw Franky in front of the business end, she said, "Please, no."

I could barely see Ruby's look of pleading terror because of the blood in my eyes. I swallowed some more of the blood in my mouth and used my free hand to pull a bit of my shirt across my eyes. The second of blindness was what David was waiting for. I heard him slide off the floor while the shirt scraped the blood off my face. I gave David a second to get up, knowing that like most people, he would use his hands to get off the ground. There would be a split second when his arms had just finished their push and his legs were taking over. As the shirt fell away, I saw my opening. The butt of the Glock hit David in the temple. He was three-quarters of the way to his full height, with his hands still below his waist, when the blow to the head sent him tipping into the wall. His head and shoulders put a hole in the drywall and then the floor caught him.

I put the gun back on Franky and said, "Put your cards on the table, Ruby. All of them."

Ruby rubbed the tears off her cheeks. "I heard that you were back in town. I remembered your uncle's place, so I looked there first. I knew you wouldn't help me, not on a job like this, but I needed you. I needed someone who would be able to rob the truck without a whole crew."

"A crew would be harder to kill," I said.

Ruby nodded. "I knew you wouldn't sign on, not unless you needed something. So I called the police and told them about the house."

169

NEVER PLAY ANOTHER MAN'S GAME

I wanted to pull the trigger. Put Franky out of his misery and watch Ruby dive head first into hers. My finger tensed on the trigger, and it hovered between life and death. I reluctantly chose life.

Ruby kept talking. "I'd been using the cancer con to get into cancer clinics and hospital rooms, but I knew that it wouldn't be enough to get you on board. Too much like your uncle. No feelings in you; none human, anyway."

"So why bother telling me David here was my cousin Rick?"

"So you'd think I was trying to use your emotions to get what I wanted. It's like making a bad play for your watch when what I really want is your wallet. If you thought you had me figured out, you wouldn't be so suspicious of the job. You might not feel, but you're greedy like everyone else. I needed you to see the job and decide you wanted it for the money. I let you think I was trying to con you with family when I was really pulling on your need for money. The cancer kept you from wondering about the serendipity of me offering you a house at the exact time you needed one. No one suspects cancer patients of doing anything wrong; believe me, I know. People in those clinics tell me things that they wouldn't say to anyone else because they're too busy pitying me to think I could ever be up to something. Even when I stand outside the clinic smoking, no one ever says a thing. They think I deserve the cigarette, like I've earned it. They never hassle me because cancer gets everyone a free pass."

It was what I had pieced together. Ruby had developed a complex, layered con that had me doing things for her without realizing that she was pulling my strings.

"You always were the best con I ever knew, Ruby. But robbing an armoured car isn't a con, and killing people isn't stealing a wallet. You thought you were the smartest

MIKE KNOWLES

chick in the room and you thought you could play another man's game as well as your own." I looked at Franky and then at David still out on the floor. "Turns out you weren't as smart as you thought you were."

"It wasn't supposed to be like this."

"Too late for supposed to be. It is what it is and now you need to deal with it."

"And how am I supposed to do that?"

"The same way I have to," I said. "We need to steal a hell of a lot of money."

CHAPTER TWENTY-SEVEN

"Money? What good is money now?"

"Makes the world go round, Ruby. Turns shit into apple pie if you have enough of it. With money, you can get out of the city forever. Without it, the cops will find you a few days after the bikers finish with you."

"And where do we get this money? I don't think next Friday's truck will be so easy."

"Your boy paid off his debts in cash last night?"

Ruby nodded.

"Well, that's a start."

Ken brought David to with some smelling salts from a medical bag on the floor beside Franky's futon.

"My head fuckin' hurts."

"Well, my stomach and my wallet are empty," I said. "And since I have the gun, we'll deal with my problems first. Ken, get me something to eat while David tells me where the money went."

Ken protested, but Ruby pushed him to do it. She knew

she needed the money back, and that she couldn't get it without me.

"Do I have to tell you what will happen if you call the cops, Ken?"

Ken stopped in the doorway, looked at me, and then shook his head. I told him anyway. "They'll arrest Ruby and your kids. The bikers will get David and Franky, if he pulls through, on the inside, and Ruby will get to rot until she gets cancer for real."

"I know that," he said.

He started to turn for the door; what I said next was a verbal speed bump that stalled him on the threshold. "You get it in your head to come up here with more than a sandwich and it will be worse. Twice now, you and your family have tried to kill me. You go for a hat trick and I'm going to start killing back. Starting with the vegetable." I lifted the Glock off my knee and extended it towards the bed. Ken followed the straight line from the barrel of the gun to his unconscious son. "Understand?"

Ken's right eye fluttered. "Start with? You put two bullets in my son."

Ruby sprinted across the room putting herself between the gun and her son. "Just do what he says, Ken. Please."

Ken whirled towards Ruby, ready to unload on her, but her sobs deflated the sudden burst of anger he was riding.

"I don't have anything left. No more cons or scams. I can't save him. I thought I could, and look what happened." Ruby stepped back and took Franky's limp hand. "Look what happened to my baby because of me."

"This is on me, Ma, not you," David said.

The look Ruby gave him let everyone know that she wasn't taking all of the blame. It was an eighty-twenty split, but the twenty on Ruby's shoulders was a heavy fucking weight that the frail old woman couldn't add any more grief to.

"I let it happen. I should have known better." She looked me in the eye. "I should have known. I can't lose any more, Ken. We need to get out of this. Whatever it takes. So please, just do as he says."

Ken's shoulders slumped and I could see that he was spent. He had no fight left in him, not for her, not for me. The old man nodded to Ruby and walked out of the room while I got David to start telling me about the money. He had been lying low for a week waiting for the job. He owed two hundred grand to the triad and it was due seven days ago. He had been a regular at underground poker games in Toronto for a while and, according to him, he was good. It didn't matter if I believed him; the triad believed him enough to let him sit at the table for the high-stakes games. He hit a bad streak and ended up in the hole to some very bad and very greedy people.

He had been down with the triad before, not to the tune of a few hundred grand, but he had been treading water in the red. He had done some armed robbery — gas stations, convenience stores, even a few banks — to get flush. Hearing him brag, while barely concealing a smug smirk, about his stick-up work explained the steel nerves I saw on the day of the robbery. David was a degenerate with a skill set. The money from the hold-ups was never enough to pay off his debts entirely, but the few thousand he picked up on each job always bought him more time to cover his losses. The triad had been smart: they didn't kill David, or even mess him up a little; they just let him rack up more and more debt. Big River kept on giving him time to pay them back because they, like David, were gamblers. But unlike David, their bet had paid off.

"Two hundred grand. That's all the truck had?"

"Just a bit over that. There wasn't a double load this week," David said. "Guess they fixed the trucks early."

David took two hundred grand to the home of Yang Tam. Yang was a big name in the Big River triad. He was an underboss who ran everything illegal west of Toronto. I had heard his name attached to a bust of a hundred-million-dollar drug ring that ran from Hamilton to Niagara a few months back. I'd heard his name, but the police never even knew he existed. The cops only managed to snag middle management and put a temporary kink in Yang's operation. It took him less than a month to be back in business again.

"You know where he lives?" I asked.

"He has a house up on the Escarpment. It's a huge mansion on a private road."

"Not in Toronto?"

"He runs all kinds of illegal shit between Toronto and the border, and Hamilton is in the middle of everything. He bought a place here and a few businesses — legit ones that make him look respectable on paper. That's about the only place he would look that way. If you ever met him, it wouldn't matter if on paper it said he gave millions to charity, you'd know he was dirty."

"So you took him the money and that was that? He didn't ask you where you got it?"

"He did, but I just told him that I got lucky at some tables in Buffalo. I told him I had to play in a bunch of games to make the money back. That's why I was a week late."

"He believe you?"

"If he didn't, he didn't say. He wasn't mad or anything. He was fine. He let me sit in on a game at the house."

"Why wouldn't he? You just paid him two hundred grand. Everyone loves a shit player with deep pockets.

How long did you play?"

"All night," David said.

"You came here right after?"

He nodded.

"How much did you lose?"

David didn't have an answer.

"How much?" Ruby demanded.

"Fuck, Ma. Eight, alright. I lost eight. It's no big deal. We had ten left over from the job."

"You lost eight thousand after we just paid off two hundred?" Ruby broke off into a stream of Chinese that I couldn't follow. I could tell from the speed, volume, and look on David's face that it wasn't a happy conversation.

"I'm sorry, Ma. I thought my luck had finally changed. We got the money and paid off Yang. I thought I could make a little cash."

"What is he talking about?" Ken asked from the doorway. He was carrying a sandwich and a bottle of water.

I took the food out of his hands before I said, "David lost eight Gs in a poker game with the triads last night."

"What the hell is wrong with you?" Ken charged across the room and began slapping his son. I was glad I had taken the food before I said anything. I tried to take a bite of the peanut butter sandwich while I watched the beating, but my loose teeth would have none of it. I switched to the water and drank slowly, enjoying the way it got rid of the taste of blood in my mouth.

Ken eventually tired of hitting his kid and flopped down onto the floor. He looked worse than David. The drinking, lack of sleep, one child almost dead, and the other an uncontrollable fuckup had taken a severe toll.

"What time did the game end?"

David rubbed at his cheeks; they were going red from the slaps.

NEVER PLAY ANOTHER MAN'S GAME

"Answer him!" both parents yelled.

"I don't know. Around four, I guess. It ended around four."

"Everyone leave with you?"

"Yeah, we all walked out the door at the same time."

"What about security? Yang have any guys stay behind?"

"At his house? He doesn't have security living with him. They walked out with us, too. Yang locked the door and turned off the lights before we even got in our cars."

"Alright," I said.

"Alright what?" Ruby asked.

"The money is at the house. He didn't move it last night, but you can be damn sure he'll move it today."

"Why?"

I used the napkin under the sandwich to dab at my forehead — it came away bloody. "Ken, do think you could stitch me up?"

The old medic squinted at me and then nodded. He got up and lumbered to his bag while I talked. "Think about it, Ruby. You got two hundred grand from a guy who gives you a bullshit story about where he got it and the next day you see his face on the news. Are you going to keep the money at your house?"

"No," Ruby said.

"That's right, because if David gets pinched, Yang knows he'll give up where the money is in a heartbeat. Giving the money back means reduced jail time. So Yang has one choice."

"Move the money," Ruby said.

The needle broke the skin and I felt the thread pull through. "He has to move it out of his house and down that private road."

"So what do we do?"

"That depends. You still have the van?"

"It's out back — stashed in the trees out behind the field," David said. "We drove Franky straight here in it."

"You have an Internet connection?"

Ken said yeah as he tied off the stitches in my eyebrow.

"Then we get started."

CHAPTER TWENTY-EIGHT

"You figure Yang is an early riser?"

David looked at me. "No, he works nights like I do."

"Yeah, but you just paid him two hundred grand, so you're not all that alike despite the similar hours. Was he drinking last night?"

"A bit."

"Yawning?"

"Yeah, I saw him do that three or four times near the end of the game."

"Alright, so we assume he went to bed after you left and that he hasn't yet read the paper or watched the news," I said as I finished wiping my face with the wet towel Ruby had gotten for me. My face was tender all over from the beating. I put the towel down on the computer desk and opened up Google. I found Hill Street, the private road Yang lived on, on Google Earth and zoomed in enough to see cars on the driveway. The road was off Upper James Street just before the Escarpment access wound down the side of the mountain to the city core. The private road was just before the hill. I used Google street view to move up and down Upper James. The private road wasn't mapped, but I could look down it from the main road. It looked to be maybe a few kilometres long and two lanes wide. Google had taken shots of it in the summer so I had to imagine it without the beautiful foliage.

I backed up the virtual street, pausing every few seconds to look left and then right. I found a parking lot belonging to a bar about a click from the private road. What I had planned would take only a few hours, making the bar parking lot perfect. It looked like the kind of small place that would open late in the afternoon but not get busy until a game started on TV.

I went over the plan and made sure everyone had it all straight. Ruby and David were on board, or so they said. The money would be cut in half. I wasn't taking the bigger slice for them trying to kill me — the extra money was for getting them out of the city to a place the law or the bikers would never find them. Ruby and David might have been thinking about trying to kill me again, but that would have to wait until after we had the money. No matter what, they needed the cash and I was the only way they were going to get it.

MIKE KNOWLES

CHAPTER TWENTY-NINE

We were in the parking lot of the Brass Lantern. The bar was dark and there were no cars out front, or with us out back. We were in the van waiting on a call. Ruby sat beside me staring at the phone on the dashboard while I watched the road.

She and David had followed me in the van while I drove the Range Rover back to Sully's Tavern. I crammed the Range Rover into a parking space, hitting the brakes only when the sound of compressing metal garbage cans could be heard over the stereo. I left the Range Rover behind the bar where Steve would be sure to find it, and took the wheel of the van from Ruby. I got behind the wheel of the van and drove to Upper James. We let David out at the entrance to the private road — he needed to be on foot to do his part. Ruby climbed back up front and we drove to the bar, less than a kilometre away.

I didn't say anything to Ruby while we waited. She seemed okay with the silence at first, but after a while something in her felt the need to try to fill the void. "I'm sorry."

When she got nothing from me, she went on.

"I mean it. I didn't want it to be like this. I had no choice. The triad would kill David. I had to do something to help him. Look at me, Wilson," she said as she pulled her kerchief off her scalp. "I did this to my head so I could con dying people out of their homes and possessions. This wasn't how I wanted my golden years to be. I wanted so much more than this, but my demons wouldn't let me have a better life. Worse, they wanted David, too. My demons weren't satisfied with me. They wanted him because I was picked clean. I had to try and save him. I had to. I thought if I helped him get out of debt, he would learn. He would be able to overcome the demons and get away."

I thought of the eight grand he already lost. What would Ruby have to do next time to pay off what he owed?

"You're thinking he didn't learn anything, aren't you? I know that. It hurts me to see that he is stuck on that path, almost as much as it hurts me to look at Franky lying on that bed. But what can I do? I had no choice. He is my son. I don't want him to end up like me. You have to understand that. You have to."

The phone rang and the noise shut her up. I picked up the phone and said, "Yeah?"

I listened to David and then hung up the phone. "Someone just pulled into the driveway. David saw them get out. He recognized them as three of Yang's bodyguards."

"He's moving the money," Ruby said.

I nodded. Ruby didn't try to talk to me after that. She put the kerchief back on and waited with her eyes glued to the phone. I waited, like Ruby, for the phone, but I didn't stare at it. I waited still as the frozen puddles on the concrete. I knew what was coming. I wasn't anxious or worried. I was ready. The phone rang three minutes later. This time I didn't have to say anything. When the phone touched my ear, I heard David say, "It's on."

I closed the phone and started the van. We drove out of the lot and got on Upper James without slowing down. We had less than a kilometre to our turn. I rammed the pedal down and watched the speedometer climb. I took the right onto the private road without using the brake. I just took my foot off the gas for a second and then shoved it back to the mat. Ruby tipped into me and then slammed back against the other side of the van.

"You said you didn't want it to be like this. That you had no choice," I said.

"Jesus, Wilson, slow down! The car is right there!"

Ruby pointed at the BMW coming towards us. We weren't slowing to block the road like we were supposed to. The van was merging into their lane at 80 kilometres an hour like a guided missile.

"I had a choice, Ruby, and I made it. I just wanted you to know that I wanted it to be this way."

Ruby was too busy clawing at the wheel to notice the grin on my face. At the last second, I let her have the wheel. I was more interested in her seatbelt. I unclicked it and a moment later I felt the air leave my chest.

CHAPTER THIRTY

The world returned in phases like the tide slowly coming in. First, I heard the horn — a constant blaring sound. The sound faded as the tide went out and then it came back as the water crept further up shore. The horn was paired with the smell of smoke. It was an acrid smell born from different automobile fluids mingling and burning. Finally, the sound and smell was joined by the sight of the BMW. The van had hit the smaller car as it tried to swerve out of the way. The corner of the black sedan had been completely flattened by the front bumper of the van. The impact sent shockwaves through the BMW; the metal of the hood bloomed out like an empty pop can that had been stepped on, leaving the car unrecognizable.

I looked to my right and saw no one in the passenger seat. The windshield told me where Ruby had gone. The hole above the dashboard was about the size of a small human body. The impact had started Ruby's career as a human cannonball. It was a one-time gig.

The space between my seat and the steering wheel had

been compressed as if a much smaller person had been driving and I had forgotten to readjust the seat. I unbuckled myself and slipped my legs out from under the dashboard. When my feet touched the ground, I had to use the door to keep myself on my feet. The world was spinning and threatening to throw me to the ground if I didn't hold on to something. I shook my head and blinked hard enough to make my eyes water. Within a few seconds, the merry-go-round I was on slowed down and my equilibrium returned. I let go of the door and drew the Glock.

The BMW had three passengers inside. The two riding up front wore their seatbelts, but the restraints didn't save them. The seatbelts just held the two men in place so that the dashboard could crush them. The man in the back seat was still breathing. He saw me through the side window and then he noticed the gun in my hand. He started frantically pawing around the back seat, looking for what had to be a gun of his own. I put a bullet in the side of his head.

The sound of the gunshot was louder than the horn, but the horn had stamina and it immediately took over again. The horn's song picked up a percussion section when bullets started hitting the BMW. I went low, using the vehicle for cover, while David emptied what was left in the AK-47 from the trees he was hiding in.

The sound of metal piercing metal trailed off like the end of a rainstorm and I risked a look over the bumper. David was twenty feet back from the road with the rifle still pointed in my direction, but he wasn't looking at me — he was looking at something at the edge of the road. The something was the body of his mother. Ruby had flown thirty feet from the car wreck into a tree. From where I crouched, it looked like she had been turned inside out.

David was saying something, but I couldn't make it out over the horn. I didn't waste time trying to read his lips; I rose out of the crouch and came up from behind the trunk with the Glock in a two-handed grip. I pulled the trigger three times fast. The first and third bullet missed, but number two hit David in the side. He fell down beside the meat that was his mother — the AK still in his hands.

The shock from the car crash was gone — adrenalin had kicked in and taken over. I pulled hard on the rear door of the BMW and it gave way with a screech. I shoved the dead man over and pulled the seat release. The back seat tipped forward and I saw into the trunk. There were two duffel bags inside the dark space. I pulled each out and pushed the seats back up.

Two hundred thousand dollars in cash weighs more than you think. A bill is light on its own, but multiplied thousands of times over it becomes a challenge — especially after you just walked away from a car wreck. I put each bag over a shoulder and got up on one knee. When I looked over the trunk, I saw that David wasn't beside his mother anymore. There was only Ruby's mangled body on the ground and a trail of blood leading into the trees. Google Earth had shown me that the side of the street opposite Yang Tam's house was all forest. The trees went back a couple hundred metres and that was where I had told David to sit and watch for the money to move. The trail of blood became impossible to see as soon as it touched the dark soil under the trees. I still had ten rounds, but David had more left in the AK's spare magazine. If I stepped out from behind the car to go after him, he would have all the advantages. I didn't have the time to wait David out; the sound of the crash and the car horn had probably already alerted the neighbours and had the cops on the way. Anyone rich enough to live on a private road would be quick to call the police and the cops wouldn't waste any time responding.

NEVER PLAY ANOTHER MAN'S GAME

I moved around the BMW and slipped behind the van. Suddenly, for a second, the horn got louder like it was in surround sound. I looked around and saw Steve's Range Rover at the end of the private road. I made a break for Steve and got three steps from the van before bullets dug into the pavement around me — David was still alive. I dove back for cover beside the van and signalled for Steve to wait. I moved to the open door and leaned into the van. The engine was still alive. I pulled the gearshift into reverse and felt the rear wheel drive respond. The van rolled back five feet and then shuddered like a freezing elephant. The engine didn't have much left. I leaned into the front seat and gave the van some gas with my hand. The van picked up its pace as more gunfire from the trees shattered what was left of the windshield. I pushed harder on the gas and the van rolled faster, dragging my feet along the pavement as it towed me along with it. I got twenty feet before the engine died. I pulled the shifter into neutral and let the van coast as far as it could. When the van started to creep, I reached up and swung the wheel to the right angling the van across the street. David let loose again from the forest, but his sight line was blocked by the body of the van. I ran, hauling the bags as they slapped into my legs, to the Range Rover. Steve leaned across the seat and opened the door; the Range Rover took off the second more than half of me was inside.

I hated leaving David alive back in the trees, but the cops would be everywhere in a few minutes. I had to hope that the gut shot would do what I didn't have time for. We sped down the Escarpment into the city. On the way, we passed two cruisers with their lights on. The police cars didn't brake when they passed us — they just kept charging up the hill.

"So you got my note," I said.

Steve nodded. "You didn't have to hit the garbage cans so goddamn hard. I was already awake."

"I needed you to check out the car so you would see the note."

On the way to return the Range Rover, I had written a note on a napkin I found in a cup holder. The note just said: *Be close to Hill Street this morning. You'll know when to pick me up.*

"You owe me for the damage to the front end," Steve said. The bartender was more concerned about the dents on the car than the ones on my face. I smiled and it hurt.

"I can cover it, I think."

"What did you do with Ox?"

"I took him home. Sandra wouldn't let him leave on his own as drunk as he was."

Steve's wife was a good person. I had wondered, too many times to count, how it was that people like us knew someone like her.

"How drunk did he get?"

Steve spoke while he checked his mirrors and changed lanes. "He wouldn't stop complaining, so I told him to start drinking until I said different."

"What time did you say different?"

"I didn't. He passed out around two."

"Where's he live?"

"Nice place over in the north end."

I got Steve to give me directions and then asked him to drop me at an intersection where I saw a few cabs waiting at the lights. "Thanks," I said.

"Come by for dinner. Sandra says she hasn't seen you in a while."

I laughed at Steve. How many getaway drivers invite someone to dinner at their wife's behest? "I'll come by the bar tonight."

NEVER PLAY ANOTHER MAN'S GAME

Steve nodded and said, "Shut the door."

I slid into a cab and told the cabbie to take me to the address Steve had given me. The drive took just a few minutes to get to Ox's place. The old man lived in a beautiful two-storey that looked to be pre-war. The house was immaculately kept and had beautifully manicured shrubs and freshly tilled flower beds. It was just after nine; a time when most people would be up, but most people weren't coming off a late-night bender. I had to bang on the door for three straight minutes to get Ox to open up.

He looked like shit. His grey hair was sticking up at the back of head while the side was pressed flat to his scalp. He was wearing a stretched-out undershirt and stained boxer shorts than had ridden up on one leg. The old man's eyes were bloodshot and they only seemed able to open halfway. He kept opening and closing his mouth and his tongue made a gross sound every time he peeled it off the roof of his mouth.

"You have a nice place, Ox. Real nice."

"C'mon, man, Steve said this shit was over. I tol' him I wouldn't say a word."

Ox's breath was heinous and I had to resist the urge to step back. "Invite me in, Ox."

He opened his eyes a bit more and what he saw made him laugh. The sound hurt him and he grabbed at his head while he spoke. "You look half as bad as I feel. I gotta tell you, it's real nice to see that you got smacked around. Not fun, is it?"

"You want to see if I can make you look worse?"

He sighed and I saw his face contort as though he was about to cry. "Fine, fuckin' fine. C'mon in."

We stepped into a small mud room where I saw shoes neatly arranged on a small wooden rack. I untied my boots and put them at the end of the top row. When I stood up,

Ox said, "Are you serious?"

I shrugged and walked into his kitchen. There was no table, only bar-stool seating on one side of the kitchen island. To my left was a living room with two comfort-able- looking leather chairs, a television with a DVD player, a stereo, and a lot of books. I put the money on the floor and motioned for Ox to take a seat at the counter. Ox rubbed at his mouth with his forearm and then climbed up on the stool. He was still a bit drunk and he almost lost his balance climbing on to the stool. I unzipped the bag and took out a stack of cash bound with a thick rubber band. I tossed it to Ox and he almost fell from his perch trying to catch it. I kept him upright and picked up the money off the floor. I put it on the counter behind him and said, "Ten grand for your trouble."

"What? You're paying me ten Gs?"

"I think it's a fair amount for one night's work."

Ox ran his hand over the stubble on his jaw. "It is, but I didn't work last night. You kidnapped me."

"See it how you want. But remember, it could end like a job," I said, lifting the money, "or like a kidnapping. Your choice."

Ox picked up the cash and fanned it. "It was a pleasure working with you."

"We square, Ox?" I asked.

Ox started to answer, but instead he jumped off his stool and ran around the island. Whatever he drank last night splashed into the sink. When he finished heaving, Ox ran the tap and stuck his face under the stream. He turned off the water and looked at me with his face still dripping. "Yeah," he said, "we're square. The money more than makes us even — it makes us friends."

"In that case, I need a favour."

Ox shot me a look while he fumbled for a few sheets

of paper towel to dry off his face. "I need to watch what I say around you. You're a literal son of a bitch, aren't ya?"

"I need some transportation. You know a guy who can help with that?"

"I know plenty of guys for that."

"Yeah, but I want something that will pass being stopped by the cops."

"You still have my phone?"

I handed over the BlackBerry. Ox wiped with screen with his undershirt and scrolled through the menu. He burped something that I could smell where I was sitting and then wrote down an address on a scrap of paper he pulled from a drawer.

"Henry will have something for you. Just tell him that it was me who sent you by."

"That won't be code for him to let me ride off on a bullet, will it?"

"You are goddamn literal and paranoid. It's code to give me a kickback. He sells you a clean car on my recommendation, I get a piece. There's no money in you being dead."

"Thanks, Ox," I said.

"Give me a number where I can get a hold of you."

I gave him the number of the cell phone in my pocket. "This is all I have right now."

"Set up something more permanent. Something with an answering service. I might have work from time to time that you would be interested in."

"Thanks, Ox."

"Words mean nothing," he said, "just say thank you by leaving so I can vomit in peace."

MIKE KNOWLES

CHAPTER THIRTY-ONE

Ox's guy hooked me up with a black Honda Accord. The car looked old, but the engine had been done up right. It wasn't as good as the Volvo's had been, but it was better than stolen cars and cabs. I had just gotten back to my place when the cell phone rang. The only one still alive with the number was Ox.

"You can't really think that I want a job already. You still drunk?"

"Shut up and listen. I just heard from a guy that a certain triad heavy got ripped off this morning."

"You don't say."

"I don't, this guy does. This guy also says that the triads have a guy who knows who did the robbery."

"Uh-hunh."

"Yeah, and this thief is apparently friends with a guy who runs a bar."

I hung up the phone and dialled Sully's Tavern. Steve picked up on the first ring.

"They there?"

"Yep."

"You okay?"

"Yep."

"Sandra?"

"Upstairs."

"Tell him that I'm coming now."

"He says he wants his money."

"Tell him no problem."

I hung up and shouldered the money out the door and into the Honda. I used the cell to make a call before I got into the car and drove into a trap.

CHAPTER THIRTY-TWO

The street out front of Sully's Tavern was full of souped-up imports. Each car had bright paint jobs, spoilers, custom rims, and fat mufflers. There was also a black Porsche suv parked directly in front of the door to the bar. I found a spot on a side street and got out of the car with a duffel over my shoulder. I walked into the bar and saw that business should have been good — if anyone inside was drinking. Twelve bar stools all had asses on them. The men on the seats were closer to boys than adults. Each had spiked hair. Some accentuated it with a rat-tail, mullet, or lines shaved into the sides of their heads. Behind the bar, I saw Steve in his T-shirt reading the paper. His hair hung down over his face and he had to tilt his head to see me in the doorway. He nodded at me and went back to reading.

At a table in the corner sat three men. One was huge — Chinese, with a Bruce Lee haircut and an Arnold Schwarzenegger physique. Beside him was a short, fat man in a dark suit. He bore a resemblance to Buddha, only the chubby deity didn't sport six inches of wispy chin hair, and none of the pictures I saw ever portrayed Buddha with brown teeth. Beside the fat man sat David. He was pale, sweaty, and hunched over.

"This him?"

David nodded and the fat man took a drag on a cigarette. He motioned for me to come over as he let the smoke slowly pour out of his mouth and over his wrecked teeth. In front of the man were two Taco Bell bags. The paper bags were greasy and wrinkled. The fat man rested his cigarette on the plastic lid of his cup and took a bite out of a fat burrito stuffed with what looked to be like a whole other meal as I crossed the room. Crumbs and meat showered his suit and he brushed them away with a hand that resembled an overinflated rubber glove.

I got to the table and the muscular guy got up. He had a sawed-off shotgun in his hands. The shotgun was pointed at my stomach.

"You Wilson?" The fat man asked after a swallow.

I nodded. "You Yang Tam?"

He took a drag on the cigarette and let the smoke roll out like fog over water. "Who I am is the man you stole a lot of money from." He bit into the burrito again and more food splashed his shirt.

"Money wasn't his to give," I said.

Yang laughed. He looked like Buddha again for a second until I noticed his eyes. The cold, hard black dots set inside the fat face made him look nothing like the jolly deity. "Doesn't matter where he got it. The money was mine the second it touched my hand. And the second it left my hand, it was stolen — from me."

Yang ate the rest of the thing in his hand in one bite. Nothing fell onto his suit this time. He then dug into the second bag and pulled out something else wrapped in paper. Yang unfolded the paper and said, "You see this burrito?

I only bought one because I'm watching my weight, but I missed breakfast this morning because, well you know why, and I'm still hungry. This burrito was Arthur's." Yang gestured towards the muscular man beside him, using the Mexican food as a pointer. "You think Arthur is going to take it back from me? It wasn't mine. I had no right to it. You think he's going to reach over the table and take it right out from under my nose?" He looked at Arthur. "Would you even think about touching it?"

Arthur shook his head.

"Why is that, Arthur?"

"Because you'd kill me."

"I would fucking kill you if you touched *my* Taco Bell." Yang put down the food and started stroking his sparse chin hair without wiping his greasy fingers first. With his other hand, he lifted the cigarette to his mouth and took a long drag. He spoke through the smoke. "Think about that. Arthur's been with me for years. I fucking love Arthur, and I would kill him dead over ninety-nine cents of shitty Mexican food. Think about where you are in this equation. I don't know you, you killed three of my guys, and you stole the equivalent of two hundred thousand burritos from me. Two hundred thousand!" Yang slapped the fast food bag away and flicked his cigarette at me. The butt sparked against my coat and fell to the floor. I noticed in my peripheral vision that everyone at the bar had swivelled on their stools so that they could look at me.

"Maybe less money for burritos isn't such a bad thing."

The air went still in the room as everyone searched for the source of the jab. It had come from behind me, but I didn't turn my head — I was glued to the shotgun aimed at my guts. At this range, Arthur could saw me in half if he moved his finger just half an inch. His eyes were on whoever was behind me, but the gun was still looking right at my waist and his finger was still on the trigger.

The voice kept talking. "I mean seriously, you smoke and you eat that shit. You have to see the writing on the wall. How long do you expect to live?"

"Longer than you," Yang said.

The threat was serious, but the voice didn't quiver — there was only a short bark of laughter. "Heh, good one. Bartender, grab me a beer. A Rickards, if you got it."

I saw Steve look up over his paper at the man. Steve nodded like it was just a regular night, took his time folding the paper, and bent to get a bottle from the fridge under the bar. He put the beer on the counter and I finally got a chance to see who had come into the bar. The beer was picked up by a man in his fifties with short brown hair that had gone grey at the temples. He had a handlebar moustache that had started to go white under his nose and a scar on his neck running parallel with his jaw. It looked like someone had once tried to cut the man's throat. He was short, maybe five-five, and dressed in black jeans and a black trench coat over a black sweater. The man took the beer off the bar and walked away from the twelve gangsters on the stools. None of the triad tried to stop him — they were soldiers, and soldiers waited for orders.

Yang put another cigarette into his mouth and leaned back in his chair. Arthur used his left hand to go into his pocket — the right kept the shotgun on me. I watched the gun and how Arthur moved. Everything he did was burned into my brain. With one hand, he flicked the silver Zippo lighter open and thumbed a flame to life. He took his eyes off me just long enough to make sure the flame was close enough to his boss for him to light the cigarette without moving his fat neck. Yang touched the fire and Arthur immediately swung his head back to check my position. If someone had used my Before and After picture as a cereal box game of Spot the Difference, it would have taken most kids an hour to see the slight change. My hand was closer to my belt and the gun tucked underneath. Arthur put the lighter away and put his left hand back on the gun.

The short man walked up to our table and stood to my right. "Your cholesterol alone must be high triple digits. You ever get it checked, tubby?"

I had never laid eyes on the mouthy little prick before, but I had no doubt about who he was — after all, I was the one who had called him.

Yang looked around the room like he couldn't believe what he was hearing. "I don't give a shit about cholesterol. I care about getting what I want."

"Obviously," the little man said.

"Who the fuck are you, midget?"

The short man took a pull on his beer. "Midget? I bet I'm at least your height. How tall are you?"

"Five seven," Yang said.

"Maybe five seven around the middle. No way you're that tall. Let's measure back to back."

Yang almost jumped out of his chair. "Motherfucker, you are about to have the worst night of your life."

The short man pulled a chair away from another table and sat down beside me. "Maybe," he said, "but first, I want to hear more of this burrito story. So you stole the big man's food because you were still hungry, shocker, and he won't take it back because you'd kill him if he tried."

Yang said, "I think I can show you what I mean."

"In a second. Just let me ask you one thing. Would you still want the burrito if Arthur had taken it from someone else?"

"Doesn't matter who it belonged to. It's in front of me."

"I'm not questioning the physical location of the food.

I'm asking you if you'd still want it if it were, say, God's burrito."

"God's burrito?"

The little man nodded and drank some more beer. "Would you still want to eat the burrito you stole from your man here if you found out that he swiped it from God?"

"Are you fucking drunk, little man? God's burrito." Yang laughed and a second later, all of his minions at the bar joined in. It was a disturbing sight.

When the laughter died, the little man said, "I'm not drunk, and I don't mean Jesus. I mean Old Testament God. The kind of God who would rain down fire, turn rivers to blood, the kind who would kill your firstborn just to ruin your day."

"You threatening me?"

A couple of the triads got off their stools.

"No, I'm asking you if you'd still eat the burrito."

"This is pointless."

The little man drained the beer and threw the bottle across the room. The glass shattered on the opposite wall and rained jagged amber on the floor. "It's very much on point because that money belonged to someone else before you put your fat greasy hands on it. That money was the property of someone who would have no problem killing every living thing in this room."

"So you're God?" Yang said.

"No, not God, just a man who doesn't appreciate being fucked with and —"

The glasses behind the bar started to vibrate, producing a sound like a wind chime in a breeze. The room grew loud as engines roared on the street. It was the sound of machinery engineered to produce nothing but horsepower and noise. The noise grew louder as dark shapes raced past on the sidewalk outside the front window. The noise reached a deafening cacophony before it died in an instant.

"Just a man," Roland said, "a man who appreciates a little old-school biblical fire, blood, and death."

CHAPTER THIRTY-THREE

The door to the bar opened and the Forty Thieves walked in. It was as though someone had wheeled a machine to the door that spit angry men in various sizes down a conveyor belt and into the room. Each unshaven, leather-clad biker who stepped into the bar had the same hard eyes I had seen on muzzled dogs waiting to be let out of their cages to fight for money. Soon every triad had a friend wearing a patch.

"'Nother beer," Roland "The Big Dawg" Simcoe said. I bet if anyone found the Big Dawg name funny, they kept it to themselves.

One of the bikers took a beer from Steve, who actually sighed when he had to put down his paper, and walked it to Roland.

"Who are you?" Yang asked.

"You can think of me as the guy you stole the burrito from."

Yang looked at me.

"Read the jackets," I said.

I watched the fat man look from jacket to jacket. The patch showing a skeletal hand holding a wad of cash was enough for anyone to realize who they were talking to.

"So the money David —"

"Shhh, not yet," Roland said. "We're still waiting for someone."

We sat in silence for a few minutes until the door opened again. Five more men came in from the cold. The man second from the end was helped inside; his wheelchair had trouble with the steps. D.B. rolled towards the table trailed by two pit bulls. Even without the use of his legs, D.B. was still imposing. The other four bikers fanned out and each went to a corner of the bar. The dogs sauntered over to Roland and sat beside him. D.B. caught up a second later.

"Hey, Rick," he said, nodding in David's direction. You had to know D.B. to hear the hate in the greeting.

I shook my head. "It's David."

"No shit? Ruby really his mom?"

"She was."

D.B.'s eyebrow raised. He didn't miss the word *was*.

"That the money?" D.B. asked.

"It's my money," Yang barked.

"So you'd eat God's burrito then?" Roland asked.

"You're not God, you're a fucking biker."

Something in Roland's body language set the dogs on edge. They started growling at Yang. The fat triad under-boss flicked his cigarette at the dog on Roland's right. The muscular pit bull yelped while the other dog took off around the table en route to Yang's neck. Arthur moved the shotgun away from my stomach and tracked the dog. When it came all the way around the table, it would get a nasty surprise. The dog charging at Yang sparked a tidal wave of guns being drawn. Triads pulled guns and the bikers did the same. The guns were aimed everywhere

MIKE KNOWLES

because no direction was safe. It would only take one shot to set everyone off.

"Heel!" Roland yelled.

The dog never came around the table, and the shot never came. The pit bull skidded to a stop and then slunk back to its master. Arthur started to bring the shotgun back towards me, but suddenly realized that it was a terrible idea. He saw the grin on my face and then he saw the gun in my hand.

"Easy with the shotgun, muscles."

"He's a slippery one," Roland said to D.B.

"I tol' ya."

"If everyone's going to jump in the pool, I might as well get wet," I said.

Arthur had the sawed-off halfway towards me and he suddenly seemed unsure about where to point it. Finally, he chose a target that wasn't aiming anything at him. He put both barrels towards D.B.

"Aim at the gimp. That's ballsy," D.B. said.

Arthur just shrugged.

"What you did there, flicking your smoke at the dog, that says a lot about you," Roland said.

"That so?" Yang asked.

"It's the same kind of stupid thinking that must have been at work when your boy there shot up one of my people and stole that money." Roland gestured to the duffel bag that was still on my shoulder. I wished I had had a chance to put it down when I came in; the strap was digging in something fierce.

Yang flashed a look at David, who was one of the few people left in the bar without a gun in his hand. David wiped his forehead and forced out a weak cough.

"That little shit owed me money. He brought me money. I didn't ask where it came from because I don't care."

"Like the burrito," Roland said.

"Exactly."

"'Cept it ain't a fuckin' burrito, is it? It's money that belongs to us. Money your boy spilled Thieves' blood to get."

"He isn't my boy."

"Not how it looks from this angle."

"Know how I see it?" Yang asked.

The two of them were inching closer and closer to sparking an explosion, and I didn't want to be in the middle of everything when the bomb went off.

"This bag is getting heavy," I said. Mentioning the bag shut everyone up. I stepped away from the table and walked to the bar acutely aware that everyone was watching me. Even Steve had glanced up from his paper to look at me. I could swear I saw the bartender chuckle. I kept the gun on Arthur as I completed the arc around the tables to the bar. I shouldered a triad and a biker out of my way and felt the brass rail of the bar touch my back. I used my free hand to lift the shoulder strap over my head and then I let the duffel bag slip to the floor. The bag thumped loud enough to make everyone momentarily forget about the guns pointed at them. I could almost hear their minds trying to guess how much money made a noise like that. My arm tingled with the sudden return of circulation and I had to resist the urge to rub it. I picked up the bag by the handles and, with one sloppy swing, threw it on the bar.

"The burrito is on the bar. Who's going to take it home?"

Both Roland and Yang stared at the bag. Their men alternated looking at the money and their bosses. It was a bad situation — no one wanted to risk saying yes, and no one wanted to be the one to say no. With the attention off me, I walked behind the bar. If bullets started moving, under the counter would be the best place to be. I stood next to Steve and spoke quietly out of the side of my mouth. "Gun in my left pocket."

Steve slipped the revolver I took off the Russian out of my coat. No one saw him do it — everyone's eyes were glued to the bag and the two men still sitting at the table.

We were all waiting for someone to get up. Instead, D.B. wheeled away from the table towards the money. No one tried to stop him because no one wanted to be the first one shot. In his chair, D.B. was eye level with the bag. I wondered if he would be able to get it off the bar. D.B. reached out and used one hand to lift the duffel. Looking at his face, he could have been lifting a grocery bag. He put the bag on his lap and circled the chair so that he could look at the room.

"I earned this. I bled for it. It's mine." He reached behind the fat bag and pulled an Uzi from inside his coat. "Take it," he said to the room, "I fucking dare you."

A quiet quickly settled in on the bar like a pillow being forced over someone's face.

D.B. broke the silence. "I took three bullets to get this bag. Anyone want to see how far I'll go to keep it?"

No one in the bar moved. Everyone was focussed on Roland and Yang. Yang had a hard choice to make. If he wanted the bag, he had to get up and walk across the room. Yang knew, as I did, that D.B. would dissect him with the Uzi. If he decided to delegate and send one of his men for the bag, there would be two possible outcomes. A gunfight would break out and he would die — he was one of two high-value targets in the room, therefore he had the highest probability of getting shot. Or his men could disobey the order, fearing the bikers more than Yang, which would cause the triad boss to lose face. His men would never respect him after that and he would have to deal with the internal fallout that would follow.

Seconds ticked by and still nothing happened.

"Who goes first, Wilson?" D.B. asked.

I didn't have to think about it. I had already settled on the order. "The bodyguard," I said.

"Not Yang?"

"You got him, and even if you don't, when the bodyguard goes, the dogs will tear Yang apart."

"They didn't like the man's cigarette, that's for sure. So Yang gets eaten by dogs, joke sort of writes itself, then what?"

I didn't hesitate because I already knew. "Steve and I kill our way down the bar starting at the end and meeting in the middle."

"That's twelve people, bro."

I nodded, not that D.B. could see it. "Six each, but it won't really be that many. Some of your guys will get a few of them. Odds are, it will be more like three each."

"Steve, you down with this?"

Steve's answer came out as easily as if D.B. had asked him if he liked the colour blue. "Yep."

The triad all looked nervous — hearing how you're going to die has a way of doing that — but none of them took their guns off their already chosen dance partners.

Yang got out of his chair and I watched as everyone's shoulders tensed. He nodded at Arthur and the big man stood and started moving to the right. Yang walked behind him on his way to the door. The triads all took steps forward; their next steps pivoted them so that they could watch the bikers as they left. They fanned out around the door, protecting Yang, who was still inside the bar, while Arthur checked the street. When the bodyguard came back in and nodded, Yang went to leave.

"He stays," I said.

Yang got on his tiptoes and leaned to the left so that he could see me. My finger was pointed at David. He was standing just outside the cluster of men like a moon frozen in orbit. His hair was soaked with sweat and he was holding his side like he was protecting a football. Yang smiled; it was all crooked teeth and malevolence.

"You might like it better if I take him," he said.

"My man is right," D.B. said, "he should stay with us."

Yang flicked his hand dismissively, like he was brushing away a fly, and walked out. The triad followed, backing out one after another until Sully's was just a biker bar.

David, rooted in the same spot, looked panicked. I saw his lip quiver as the last triad left the bar. He was alone in front of the door looking at a lot of mean faces. His eyes moved from man to man, finding no safe haven. He finally looked at me and when he saw the grin on my face, he looked to the floor. I saw him wipe at his eyes and then turn around. Ruby's kid crawled into a booth along the back wall and buried his head in the crook of his elbow.

All of the Thieves looked happy except for Roland. He was still sitting in his chair with a scowl on his face. Instead of the Big Dawg, it was D.B. who had stood up to Yang. In a gang where balls and attitude were everything, Roland had just moved down a notch while D.B. climbed over him. But Roland wasn't stupid — he knew the men in the room loved D.B. and that once the story about him facing down the triad got out, and embellished as stories do, he would be worshipped as legend. Eventually, Roland stood up and put on a smile that almost looked genuine. Behind the smile, I knew his mind was dreaming about all of the ways he would pay back D.B. for outshining him.

"Now that the fucking slants are gone, let's get something to drink." Roland's voice sounded as genuine as his smile.

The bikers all yelled their approval and the mob turned to face Steve and me.

"Who's paying?" Steve asked.

"Just pour, little man, and be happy that we ran off the Chinamen for you."

Steve didn't move. It didn't matter that we had almost been in the middle of a hurricane of bullets a few minute before. Steve wasn't about to roll over for the Forty Thieves. My friend wasn't like Yang — he was fearless and had no problem with killing or dying. It wasn't that he was braver than the triad underboss; he was just crazier. Outside of D.B., none of the bikers knew Steve, and the anticipation of a twenty-on-one fight had them buzzing with adrenalin. I made eye contact with Roland. It took a few seconds for his brain, the part that was all instinct, to understand me. He got the message — as soon as it started, he was first to go. I would make sure that he died no matter what. But Roland didn't back down this time. He had lost enough respect for one day.

Shouting started, but D.B. quieted everyone down when he slammed a brick of cash on the bar.

"You boys stood up with me. Seems only fair that I get you drunk off your asses."

There was a loud roar of approval from the bikers, and I saw Roland sneer in D.B.'s direction. He had lost to his second in command again. Not only would he have to contend with stories of D.B.'s bravery, but there would be tales of his generosity, too.

Steve took the cash and set up the bikers while I watched D.B. roll over to Roland. Roland took a chair and spoke close to D.B.'s ear. After a minute, D.B. rolled away from the table and motioned for me to come over and speak with him.

"Ballsy move calling Roland like that," he said.

"Sometimes the safest place on the road is behind a car wreck."

"You're not safe yet. Roland wants to talk to you."

"About the rest of the money?"

"He knows there had to be more than this in an armoured car and he wants it."

"You keeping your share?"

"It's mine, bro."

"So he wants my share then."

"I told him you won't give it up."

"But he still wants it," I said.

D.B. nodded. I patted the huge biker's shoulder and walked over to Roland's table. The pit bulls were lying on the floor beside Roland's chair. Their ears twitched as I got closer and their huge, cinderblock-shaped heads lifted off the floor. I looked at each dog and thought about how fast I would be able to get the Glock out.

"Scary, aren't they?" Roland said. "Scarier still when you think about the fact that if I say one word, just one, they'll tear you apart."

I walked to the other side of the table and put my hands on the back of a chair.

"One word," Roland said. "What could you do?"

"Honestly?"

Roland raised his eyebrows.

"The dogs are both on your right, so they'll come at me from that side. Shortest distance between two points is a straight line. One of them isn't going to take the long way for strategy. Strategy isn't in their DNA. I'll put the chair in their way to slow them down an extra second and then I'll put a bullet in each of their big heads."

"You are a hard man, aren't ya?"

I didn't say anything.

"Rich man, too."

I still had nothing to say.

"Almost half a mil' is what D.B. figured. That's a lot of money. Couldn't fit all that in a duffel bag. Even if it is a big bag like that."

"Wasn't that much," I said.

"How much then?"

"Enough."

"Split two ways, I bet it is."

The dogs were still on the floor; both held me in the sights of their cold unblinking black eyes.

"Way I see it," Roland said, "I should get a cut."

"That so?"

"I've been in the job since the start. Guns for the job came from one of my contacts. So did the cars, I bet. More important, you used my guy, my best guy, and you got him hurt. I should be compensated for the help and the loss, not to mention for running off the slants."

"Guns and cars were paid for. Nobody did anything for free. D.B. signed on for the job. He's a big boy, he knew the risks. That was on him, not me. As for running off Yang, it looked like D.B. did all the heavy lifting."

Roland looked over at D.B. Everyone was patting him on the back and drinking shots with him. He looked back at me with a snarl on his face.

"I could make you cut me in."

"This isn't like taking lunch money off a sixth-grader, Roland. I'm not going to hand you some cash to keep you from waiting for me after school. You want my lunch money, you have to reach across that table and take it. So if you're feeling froggy, jump. If not, walk away, because talk like that is going to lead somewhere."

"You're in a room full of my boys, tough guy."

"Doesn't change a thing," I said. "If you're going to rip me off — you'll kill me. Same thing David tried, same thing we'll do to him." David heard me from his booth and I heard him start to sob. "If that's the way it's going to be, I'm going to kill you first. I'll die next, probably, but you'll

MIKE KNOWLES

be holding my place in line to meet St. Peter." I edged the pistol out of my pocket just enough for Roland to see my finger on the trigger. "That's the thing about fucking with people who have nothing to lose — they always manage to take something with them when they die."

"Everything cool?" D.B. had rolled back to the table.

I looked at Roland. "Is it?"

He gave it some thought. A lot of the thinking was done while he stared at the hand holding the gun in my pocket.

"Let me get one of those shots!" Roland yelled. He got up, leaving me with D.B. and the dogs. Roland walked into the crowd of men at the bar and was welcomed with offered drinks and slaps on the back.

"Keep an eye on him," I said. "He drinks enough, he might get a stupid idea in his head."

"He has plenty of those already." D.B. rolled away; the dogs silently watched him go. Their posture betrayed their eagerness to follow, but they stayed put — so did David.

I walked over to the booth on the wall. "Enjoy the party, David. We'll settle up later."

David lifted his head off the table and looked at me with red eyes. His skin was pale and covered in sweat and he was shaking like there was an earthquake under his ass. Yang had gotten him enough medical attention to keep him alive, but he wouldn't stay that way past tomorrow unless he saw a doctor. Tomorrow was about twenty more hours than he would need. I tousled his hair and he cringed.

The party raged on until last call. Throughout the night, whenever Roland looked up from whatever he was drinking, he saw that I was watching him. Every time we made eye contact, he would give me a hard look. I watched each angy glare disintegrate as it collided with my grin. He would break the stare and find a new drink, downing some more high-proof courage so that he could try to work up enough nerve to do more than eyeball me. He never got further than looking, because even drunk he understood that no matter what happened he would go first.

David moved from the booth only once. He tried to sneak out the door when a fistfight broke out between two drunk bikers. Steve saw David move and nodded to D.B.

"Where the fuck are you going? You don't like our party?" D.B. yelled. His voice was loud enough to break up the fight. Everyone in the bar looked at the man half-way to the door. He was frozen in place like an old-time movie convict caught in the prison spotlights. David shuffled back towards the booth and three bikers met him there with a pitcher of beer. The three men held his mouth open and forced him to drink the whole thing at once. David ended up on the floor coughing the beer out of his lungs and holding his mangled guts.

A few hours later, the bikers all left at once, with D.B. as the last man out.

"How much is in the bag?"

"Hundred. Half the take."

"Don't hardly seem worth it, does it?"

I shrugged. "It's what we do."

"I suppose it is," D.B. said.

D.B. rolled to the door and paused to say goodbye to David. David, sitting in a chair next to an overturned table, wouldn't look at the huge biker. Covered in sweat, beer, and vomit, the gut-shot thief was barely conscious. He gave the small spot of floor between his feet his full attention. I closed the door behind D.B., twisted the locks, and flicked off the neon sign. When I looked back at the bar, I saw Steve roll the rubber band off his wrist and use it to tie his hair up into a samurai topknot. The wiry muscles of his neck and chest were visible above the collar of the white V-neck T-shirt he was wearing. The muscles were taut like coiled springs ready to pop, and the veins were hard like firehoses.

David had noticed the silence and he looked up from the floor. He noticed Steve — it was hard not to. The quiet little unassuming bartender was gone; all that remained was a man of the same dimensions — only this man was anything but unassuming. Steve gave off a different aura now. He had changed the same way a family pet changes when it goes rabid.

"David, your mom ever tell you about Steve?"

David shook his head.

"I didn't think so. Because if she had, you would have never brought this to his doorstep."

Steve vaulted the bar in one jump and moved across the floor to David like a shark through chum. Ruby's kid had brought men with guns to the bar. Sandra had been upstairs and had enough sense to stay there, but she could have been downstairs when the triad showed up. Sandra was the only thing that mattered to Steve. She was the only thing that kept him from becoming the kind of thing people like to think they had evolved past.

David got out of his chair and put a hand up; the other was holding his stomach, which had started to bleed through his shirt. He was grimacing and he managed to get out a "please," but that was all. Steve's forehead connected with David's nose, shutting him up. I leaned an elbow on the bar and watched the little bartender beat David to death. Blood splashed the floor, then teeth, and finally brains. Steve kept on beating the corpse, turning what was left of its humanity into pulp. I knew each blow was payback for David bringing the triad to his bar, near his wife. Later, I would help him clean up and get rid of the body. It would be a long night, but that was the burden of the living — one I was happy to bear.

NEVER PLAY ANOTHER MAN'S GAME